The Heart of Joy

A Short Story

Can true, enduring love
happen twice in a lifetime?

Large Print Edition

A Prairie Heritage, Book 8

VIKKI KESTELL

Faith-Filled Fiction™

www.faith-filledfiction.com | www.vikkikestell.com

A PRAIRIE HERITAGE,
BOOK 8

THE HEART OF JOY (LARGE PRINT EDITION)
COPYRIGHT ©2016, 2020 VIKKI KESTELL
ALL RIGHTS RESERVED
ISBN 13: 978-1-970120-25-7
ISBN 10: 1-970120-25-8

DENVER, COLORADO, 1914

Joy Michaels, grieving mother and widow, resides in an aging but remarkable Denver home: a beautiful, three-story Victorian mansion resplendent with towers, turrets, peaks, and gables and known locally as Palmer House. Palmer House—*a most extraordinary refuge for young women rescued from prostitution*.

Joy and her mother, Rose Thoresen, share the responsibilities of ministering to and mentoring the young women who live under Palmer House's roof. But now Joy faces an agonizing decision: Should she remain true to the memory of her first love or open her heart to the possibility of new love?

"I will always love you, Grant," Joy whispered, "but God has called you away, and now I must follow the path he has laid before me—even if it is not what either of us would have chosen, had we been given such a choice."

DEDICATION
For those who grieve:

To every thing there is a season,

and a time to every purpose

under the heaven.

—Ecclesiastes 3:1

and

"I anoint the good end of all things

with greater beauty

than the beginning."

—The Heart of Joy

SCRIPTURE QUOTATIONS
The King James Version (KJV),

Public Domain

COVER DESIGN
Vikki Kestell

ACKNOWLEDGEMENTS

Many thanks to

my esteemed teammates,

Cheryl Adkins and **Greg McCann**,

who give selflessly of themselves

to make each new book

the most effective instrument of

God's grace possible. I love you.

TO MY READERS

This book is a work of fiction,

what I term Faith-Filled Fiction™.

While the characters and events are

fiction, they are situated

within the historical record.

PROLOGUE

DENVER, DECEMBER 1914

Billy and Mr. Wheatley wrestled the blue spruce into its place in the corner of Palmer House's great room.

The two men, one young and strapping, the other elderly but willing (and whose white hair poked out from his head in wild, pointed tufts), tipped the evergreen into an upright position and let it settle upon its stand. The men grinned at each other and stood back to survey their work.

The tree was a generous ten feet tall, and its boughs opened wide to grace the corner allotted for it. The treetop tapered to a single, pointed spire near the high ceiling. Ample room remained between spire and ceiling, however, for Billy to crown the tree with a golden star.

"What do you think, Miss Joy?" Billy asked.

"I think it is perfect."

Joy Michaels drew in a deep breath and smiled as she did so. The scent of freshly cut spruce perfumed

The Heart of Joy

the air and spilled out the great

room's doors into the foyer and

dining room, adding to the other

delicious aromas filling the house.

Laughter echoed from the

kitchen, the happy laughter of the

young women of Palmer House

sharing in the fellowship of Christmas

baking.

She inhaled again. The spruce

tree's spicy-sappy fragrance was

distinctive: It evoked the Christmas

season in Joy's heart as no other

scent could.

I love Christmas, Joy mused, *but it has been a long time since I have been able to truly celebrate it, a long time since I have felt its perfect and momentous delight.*

While her friends adjusted the tree's stand so the spruce would remain upright and unwavering, Joy gave herself to the memories of the past months—the healing journey that began on her late husband's birthday and would culminate just two Sundays from today.

"I will always love you, Grant," Joy whispered, "but God has called you away, and now I must follow the path he has laid before me— even if it is not what either of us would have chosen, had we been given such a choice."

Joy closed her eyes and sighed, contentment and peace warming her soul. Her thoughts drifted back, to the day her heart began to heal.

Yes, it was Grant's birthday.

May 2 . . .

CHAPTER 1

DENVER,
MAY 2, 1914

Joy Thoresen Michaels swayed with the jerky stop-and-go motion of the downtown trolley. In her arms she held a large bouquet of flowers cossetted in brown paper—early roses from the gardens of Palmer House. Dazzling pinks, buttery yellows, deep crimsons, and vibrant sunset blushes peeked from the open end of her package.

She was conscious of the sweet aroma rising from the roses, as were her fellow passengers. Some turned appreciative glances upon Joy. Others nodded their gratification.

One woman, gray-haired and clad head to toe in drab, worn brown, sat across the aisle facing Joy. Her back was to the windows, as was Joy's. The woman closed her eyes, let her head fall against and rest upon the window glass, and inhaled deeply. Once. And again. Then she sighed and a tiny smile played across her careworn mouth.

The Heart of Joy

Joy looked away. *I am glad these flowers can provide a moment of solace to the weary of heart, Lord.*

She cradled the brown paper bundle with the same tender care she had lavished upon her baby boy . . . the last time she had seen him.

Edmund will be three now—not three months, but three years old. And Grant, my dear husband! How is it possible that three years have worn away since you went to be with Jesus? My aching heart cannot believe it.

The trolley jerked, its braking gears ground, and the vehicle came to a shuddering stop. Joy stepped off the car's back steps. A moment later, the conveyance shuddered again and lurched forward.

As the trolley departed, Joy looked about her. She was a block from her destination. She took a moment to twitch the peplum of her blue serge suit jacket into its proper alignment and smooth a crease from her skirt. She did not touch her wide-brimmed hat or smooth her hair—she knew she had coiled and pinned the lengthy blonde braid securely at the back of her head.

Joy stood tall, both without and within, preparing herself for the emotional ordeal ahead. With a nod, she squared her shoulders and crossed the road. Her long legs, grateful for the exercise, stretched out to the extent her confining skirt would allow and made short work of the distance.

She neared the entrance, glanced once at the sign, *Riverside Cemetery*, and passed inside its gates. Her husband's resting place was around the back of Denver's cemetery. She followed the familiar graveled road until it curved and began to trace the edge of the nearby South Platte River.

The river's water ran high with spring runoff. Joy caught glimpses of the rushing water through the trees and brush that overgrew the river's banks.

Halfway across the cemetery's breadth, she came upon an automobile parked to one side of the road. She walked on. Only yards beyond the vehicle, she turned away from the road, into the grassy park.

The Heart of Joy

Grant's simple upright marker was a few rows ahead.

She wanted to run to the headstone and throw herself upon the grass above Grant's grave. She longed more than life itself to have Grant hold her again! She needed—

Joy halted and frowned. "Who?"

A man knelt by Grant's grave, his dark head bowed in prayer. A stylish bowler hat rested on the lawn not far from him.

Joy did not approach. She waited for the man to finish.

He must have sensed her presence or, he, too, may have

inhaled the potent perfume coming from the roses Joy carried and been drawn to its source. A moment later, he stood, brushed grass from the knees of his creased trousers, and turned.

"Hello, Mrs. Michaels."

"Mr. O'Dell."

They had grown less comfortable and more formal with each other as the years had crept by.

He came nearer, close enough for Joy to notice the care in his dark eyes. "We must have had the same thought."

The Heart of Joy

Joy swallowed, bobbed her chin, and managed, "Grant's birthday." Her eyes skittered away from the man's probing gaze.

"You brought flowers," he commented.

"Yes. I . . . roses. This year's first. Grant loved roses."

"Their scent is heady testimony to Mr. Wheatley's green thumb."

Joy only nodded. She cast her eyes beyond O'Dell, toward the marker on Grant's grave.

Edmund O'Dell noticed. He shifted his hat from one hand to the other. "I will leave you to your privacy. I apologize for intruding on this sacred moment."

Joy came to herself. "There is no cause to apologize, Mr. O'Dell. I simply was not expecting to see you."

She was not expecting to see Grant's best friend? Their greatest ally in the troubles that had surrounded and swept over them three years past? Their son Edmund's namesake?

"Thank you for remembering him today, Mr. O'Dell," Joy whispered. "I-I thought I was the only one . . ."

The Heart of Joy

"I miss him, too."

Joy blinked hard against the welling tears.

She willed them away.

They ignored her efforts.

A single rebellious drop leaked out and dribbled down her cheek.

O'Dell stayed planted where he was for another uncomfortable minute before, in a quiet voice, he offered, "Would you like me to wait for you by the road? I left my motorcar there. I could see you home, if you wish it."

Joy swiped the moisture from her cheek and ventured a furtive glance up at him. What she saw undid her.

Love. Raw, deeply held, long-abiding love.

Long-suffering love.

And longing.

O Lord! What am I to do? I still love Grant . . .

Joy started at her own prayer. Well, of course she still loved Grant! What kind of silly, inane statement was that?

I will always love Grant! she declared to herself in no uncertain terms.

The Heart of Joy

Another voice replied. *Then why does Edmund O'Dell's presence unsettle you so?*

She licked her lips, terrified at the possible answer.

"Joy? Are you all right?" His concern had caused him to slip into familiar address.

Joy tried to smile and failed. "Yes, of course. I fear I am a little emotional. That is all."

But was it 'all'?

"Do allow me to drive you home. I am in no hurry; take as much time as you wish. Or, of course, if you prefer, I will leave you in peace. I have no wish to distress you. Please say the word."

Joy looked toward Grant's grave and down at the wealth of blooms cradled in her arms. Suddenly she did not relish the walk back to the trolley stop after she had laid the flowers. Did not want to endure the long wait for another trolley and the longer ride home.

Did not want to be alone with her heartache.

Did not want to be alone.

Alone.

That word summarized so much of her life these past three years.

The Heart of Joy

Taking meals in the house with Mama and the others of Palmer House—but still alone.

Catching the trolley to work each morning with her employees, Sarah, Corinne, and Billy—but still alone.

Spending long, solitary evenings in the cottage near the back of Palmer House's grounds with Blackie as her only companion.

Tossing fitfully in the bed she had once shared with Grant.

Alone, alone, alone.

Alone—for three, long years.

She was grateful for Blackie, the black-and-white shepherd-mix dog she had raised from a pudgy, curly-haired pup. His soulful devotion to her had been and remained a comfort through the long nights.

And yet . . .

As much as I adore my sweet Blackie, he cannot hold me or fill this aching void in my life.

Alone.

I do not want to be alone any longer, Joy was disconcerted to realize. More than that, she did not want to be far . . . from O'Dell's comforting presence.

What? But-but . . .

The Heart of Joy

Joy was reluctant to examine her last thought too closely, so she swept it away.

O'Dell had watched the play of emotions flit across Joy's face, had watched her clamp them down. He gave his round derby a last twirl at the end of his fingertips and slipped it on his head.

"I wish you a good day, Mrs. Michaels. Again, I apologize for intruding."

"Oh! N-no!" Joy stammered. "I mean, um, I mean, thank you for your kind offer. If-if you truly do not mind waiting . . . I would appreciate your seeing me home."

She glanced up again and saw the troubled clouds clear from his eyes.

"It would be my pleasure."

"Thank you. I should be no more than ten minutes."

"Take as much time as you need, Joy. I am in no hurry."

Take as much time as you need, Joy. I am in no hurry.

The words seemed to pulse with meaning.

Joy looked down again and nodded, and O'Dell, tipping his hat to her, trod toward the road and his waiting automobile. Joy stood blinking at the grass. Then she stepped toward Grant's headstone.

She put her handbag and the flowers to one side and knelt in front of the headstone, much as O'Dell had. With eyes squeezed closed, Joy reached for the marker. Its polished marble was icy. No matter how many times she had touched it, its penetrating cold shocked her.

I expect Grant's warmth to greet me.

I am always disappointed.

Joy's fingers traced the chiseled inscription,

Grant Aubrey Michaels
Beloved Husband and Father
_1878-1911_

She wept then. She gave herself to the flood of grief.

I wonder how many tears I have shed for Grant and Edmund? she asked herself. Is there ever an end to such mourning?

Unbidden and unwanted, a passage of Scripture answered her.

The Heart of Joy

To every thing there is a season,

and a time to every purpose

under the heaven:

A time to be born,

and a time to die;

a time to plant,

and a time to pluck up

that which is planted;

A time to kill,

and a time to heal;

a time to break down,

and a time to build up;

A time to weep,

and a time to laugh;

a time to mourn,

and a time to dance.

The verses resonated in her heart as though heralded from on high.

Joy whispered her doubts aloud. "But, Lord! Is there truly a time to laugh after weeping for so long? A time to dance after such great mourning? My heart is still wounded. Distressed. I cannot fathom 'a time to heal!' I cannot conceive it."

She sniffed, removed a hanky from her pocket, and wiped her eyes. When she was more composed, Joy reached for the brown paper package. She unrolled its length and, one shoot at a time, removed the roses.

She kissed a golden-yellow bud, half-blown, and placed it in the vase embedded at the base of the headstone. "Our love was as sunny and as constant as this flower, Grant."

Next, she selected a shoot of dewy pink blossoms. "I was but a fresh-faced girl of eighteen when we met, as innocent as these blooms. How can thirteen years have passed?" She pressed her lips to the silky buds and slid them into the vase.

Joy lifted three long stems bursting with crimson color from the paper and buried her nose in their scarlet fragrance. "These remind me of the blood of Christ, Grant. Jesus saved and cleansed us with his life's blood."

One red-budded stem. "You."

Another. "Me."

The last bloom. "And Jesus. Our love and our marriage were grounded in our fellowship in him, in our common salvation."

Only the sunset roses remained. Their petals were streaked and variegated in pinks, yellows, golds, and oranges so intense, *so vivid*, that Joy lost herself in their mesmerizing kaleidoscope.

"Such beauty," she murmured. "Such brilliance. Such was our love."

She arranged the flowers in the vase with the other roses and sat back to observe her work. The glowing sunset roses seemed to outshine the others. She tucked them a little deeper into the vase, but the effect was the same: She could not take her eyes from them.

Sunset roses.

There is a season and a time to every purpose under the heaven.

"A sunset is an ending, a conclusion. Is there also a season and a time for a sunset, Lord?"

A voice seemed to call from the breeze. *I anoint the good end of all things with greater beauty than the beginning.*

"Is there a good end ahead for me? Is there, truly, Lord?"

Joy bowed her head and, although she acknowledged in her heart that Grant could not hear her, she spoke to her husband anyway.

The Heart of Joy

"Grant, my love. How I miss you! Every day I feel your absence as surely as I ever felt your presence. Three years have passed, and I still grieve for you. Three long years, and I do not even have our son to care for, to comfort me.

"And now something . . . something is changing. I do not understand it; I do not know where it will lead. I-I do know, though, how much you loved and trusted our dear friend, Mr. O'Dell. You loved and trusted him . . . to the point of naming our son after him when you knew you were dying."

A sob clogged Joy's throat. "Mr. O'Dell has spent these years searching for our baby. He has never complained or uttered a word of discouragement. He has been our—*my*—strong arm, my ally and support. And I know he has . . . feelings for me. If-if I were to give him any encouragement at all—"

Joy could not finish, could not voice—not to Grant nor to herself— what might come. Instead, she wiped her face again and spoke to her God.

"Father, I know you love me, and I trust in that love. Lead me,

The Heart of Joy

Lord, in paths of righteousness for your name's sake. I commit to you: Where you lead, I will follow."

Joy stood to her feet and smoothed away the wrinkles on her skirt, flicked away the bits of grass. She carefully, methodically, folded the brown paper and tucked it into her handbag.

Once more, she placed her hand on the marble headstone. Rubbing the smooth surface under her fingers, Joy gave the headstone a last caress.

"I love you, Grant Michaels. I will always love you, but I hear our

Lord whispering that the times and seasons are changing. Perhaps I must change, too."

O'Dell watched the tender farewell from the road, saw Joy square her shoulders and stride toward him. As she drew closer, he noted her reddened eyes and the blotchy patches on her cheeks. Nevertheless, she attempted to smile as she reached the edge of the road.

"Thank you for waiting for me, Mr. O'Dell."

O'Dell lifted his hat by way of greeting. "It was my pleasure."

The Heart of Joy

He opened the passenger door and handed her inside, then went around to the driver's side and climbed in. His 1910 touring car from the now-defunct Bergdoll automakers was not the newest or shiniest motor car running around the cobbled streets and dirt roads of Denver, but in O'Dell's role as head of the Denver Pinkerton office, the 30-horsepower auto, with front and back seats, was a godsend, an essential tool to his trade.

Not sure how I managed without it before.

Today he was doubly glad for the automobile. "Are you comfortable? Hat secure?" The car sported a partial front window and a canopy that extended above the seats and down the back, but the remainder of the auto was open to air rushing by at a brisk fifteen-mile-an-hour clip.

Joy tested the wide brim that shaded her face. "I believe so."

Her sleek, wheat-colored braid, wound about itself and pinned at her neck, filled the underside of the hat's straw and tulle. O'Dell had trouble tearing his gaze from her

The Heart of Joy

lovely hair—until he saw her watching him—watching him with a knowing expression.

"Harrumph." He cleared his dry throat and started the engine.

Am I mistaken, or is something different, Lord? Are things changing? he asked silently. *After these many years?*

They rode in silence, but it was a companionable silence. Soon they drove out of the relative peace and quiet of the cemetery and its neighborhood and into the cacophony of afternoon traffic flowing through downtown Denver.

Automobiles roared down the narrow streets, their drivers honking at passing acquaintances, at the friends who strolled the walkways along the boulevards, at the traffic snarls engendered by the confluence of horse-drawn conveyances and motorized vehicles.

Joy perked up and pointed. "Oh, look! There is Tory Washington!"

O'Dell tipped his hat to the elegant woman conversing on the wide walkway in front of her establishment, *Victoria's Fashions*.

The Heart of Joy

Tory's smart, picture-perfect attire was the best advertisement for her chic designs and gowns. One slender, gloved hand waved a greeting to Joy and O'Dell.

"It never fails to amaze me," O'Dell confessed, "how changed the young ladies we, er, 'removed' from Corinth are. How successful and happy they have become."

O'Dell was referring to the girls and young women Joy and her mother, Rose, had rescued when they lived in the little mountain village above Denver.

On that memorable night, O'Dell, a party of fellow Pinkerton agents, and a contingent of U.S. Marshals had helped terminate the bogus employment scheme by which evil men had kidnapped and ensnared the girls. They had liberated the girls and young women from forced prostitution.

Tory Washington had been one of those young women.

Not long after the Corinth showdown, an elderly Denverite, Martha Palmer, had given to Rose and Joy the house her husband had built three decades before.

The Heart of Joy

The house had been sitting empty for years and had suffered much from neglect, but its three stories and many bedrooms were exactly what Rose and Joy had prayed for.

What they had needed.

Some of the girls rescued from Corinth had gone home to be reunited with their families. Those who had no homes or family to whom they could return had come to live at Palmer House under Rose's healing ministrations. In the years since, Denver churches had recommended—and were still referring—other women in similar straits to Palmer House. To Rose and Joy's welcoming arms.

Within the safety of Palmer House's walls, mother and daughter poured love on these wounded souls, shared Jesus with them, prayed over them as they healed, and labored to prepare the women for honest work—work that allowed them to envision and achieve independent and self-sufficient futures.

Joy answered O'Dell, "Grant called them our 'girls from the mountain.' And I could not agree more with your assessment. Only

The Heart of Joy

God can restore a devastated life so completely."

Soon they were out of heavy traffic and into a well-heeled residential area. O'Dell eased his car up to the curb of an immense corner lot. He jumped from his seat and raced around the car to open Joy's door for her.

Again, she fixed him with that look—partly shy, partly knowing. A bit questioning? And most definitely skittish.

Wary.

Afraid.

He moistened his lips and—the remnant of an old habit—patted his breast pocket where he used to carry his cigars. But that was before.

Before Jesus.

She noticed his action and whispered, "Old ways crop up at the strangest times, do they not? When we are nervous."

"Are we nervous, Mrs. Michaels?" The words flew from his mouth before he could prevent them.

Joy shifted her feet and circumvented his question with a hastily crafted query of her own.

The Heart of Joy

"May I take your arm, Mr. O'Dell?"

O'Dell snapped to attention. "Certainly." They took the few steps to the gate of Palmer House. He opened the gate, and they walked through it and up the walk at a leisurely pace toward the porch. There they stopped, and O'Dell released Joy's arm.

He hesitated and then said, "I am glad I was able to share Grant's birthday with you. I know how hard it had to have been for you. I pray my presence there was a help and not an intrusion."

"Your presence has never been an intrusion, Mr. O'Dell." Joy was just being honest. With him.

With herself.

She took a deep breath. "Perhaps . . . perhaps you might join us for dinner this evening? Nothing special. Only ordinary, midweek fare."

To hide his surprise, O'Dell teased, "Are you not required to give Marit and Breona at least a twenty-four-hour notice?"

Palmer House's cook and housekeeper were legendary sticklers for propriety.

The Heart of Joy

Joy laughed—a real, uninhibited laugh. "I have a feeling they will not complain much."

O'Dell nodded and smiled in return. He could not help himself—and his gaze probed hers, looking, wondering, hoping for a sign. "Well, then. I leave them to you. Until this evening."

Joy's laughter dissolved. In its place appeared that same shy, fearful knowing.

"Yes, um . . . very well." She might just as well have been agreeing to a doctor's injection for all the lack of enthusiasm she conveyed.

She opened her mouth, perhaps to rescind her invitation—but O'Dell gave her no opportunity to do so. He raised his hat and spun on his heel, forestalling such an action.

He was halfway to the gate before she could assert her qualms or retract her invitation.

No, my dear, O'Dell thought. *We have begun now, and I shall press my suit hereafter.*

CHAPTER 2

Joy closed the front door behind her and leaned against it. Her heart was hammering.

She was breathless.

Panicked.

O Lord! What have I done?

Rose, hearing the door open and shut without any subsequent footsteps in the entryway, left her desk in Palmer House's great room and went to investigate.

"Why, Joy! Is everything all right?"

Joy laughed, and a tiny note of hysteria tinged her laughter. "I am not sure, Mama."

As she spoke, soft paw pats and the clicking of nails on the parquet wood of the foyer pattered toward them. Blackie, roused from his bed in the kitchen, raced to greet Joy. He skittered to a stop, tail thumping the floor, and grinned up at her.

Joy bent and rubbed Blackie's ears and muzzle. "Good boy, Blackie. Did you miss me? Did you have a nice day with Will and Charley?"

The Heart of Joy

Will and Charley were Billy and Marit's two young sons.

Rose smiled. "The weather was lovely today. The boys and Blackie played outside all morning. They explored every inch of the grounds together. All three were worn to a frazzle by lunch time—and all three required naps."

Rose, resolved on discovering the reason for her daughter's strange entrance, pursued her quest from a different direction. "Today is Grant's birthday, is it not? Did you take roses to his grave today? I thought I saw you cutting some this morning before you left for your shop."

"Um, yes, to both questions." Joy made that odd, strangled sound again. "You will never guess who was at the cemetery when I arrived."

Rose put her head to one side and considered her daughter. "Hmm. Someone was already there? I suppose I might venture to assume it was Mr. O'Dell?"

Joy nodded her head, but the anxious shakiness inside remained—fixed and quivering. "Yes, it was Mr. O'Dell. He remembered it was Grant's birthday, and he, um, he kindly offered to drive me home."

"I see." Rose did not see, but a tiny hope percolated in her heart. "And?"

"Yes. Well . . . that is . . . I-I . . ." Joy's sentence faded into oblivion.

"Joy."

Rose employed that age-old tone, the one all mothers perfect. She used that certain and uncanny ability to utter Joy's first name and, into a single syllable, imbue the weight of her full name: Joy Again Thoresen Michaels.

"Joy."

Joy dithered and then spit out her response. "I, um, I-I invited Mr. O'Dell to dinner this evening."

"Ah." Rose kept the smile that bloomed in her heart from reaching her face.

Joy blushed. "No, Mama. Not 'ah.' It is only dinner; that is all. He has often taken dinner at Palmer House."

"Not for quite some time, if my recollections are correct."

The Heart of Joy

Joy shrugged her shoulder. "I was merely being polite."

Rose raised one brow. "I see. Well, you had best let Marit know. It is half-past four."

"Yes. I should do so."

Joy dreaded "doing so."

Why, I shall adopt a simple, nonchalant tone. Something ordinary and customary, such as, 'I happened upon Mr. O'Dell' or 'Mr. O'Dell and I encountered each other quite by chance—and so, of course, I extended an invitation.'

That will serve.

Pursing her lips, she brushed by her mother and strode toward the kitchen, Blackie at her heels.

But when Joy pushed through the swinging door, her courage—and all her prepared words—dropped into her shoes: Not only were both Marit and Breona in the kitchen, so also were Marit's husband, Billy; Palmer House's caretaker, Mr. Wheatley; and two of Palmer House's girls, Gracie and Olive. Billy had his and Marit's younger son, Charley, on his lap while he and Mr. Wheatley sat at the kitchen table and peeled potatoes into an enameled pan.

The Heart of Joy

Conscious that every eye had turned toward her, Joy still stared at Charley. Her eyes devoured him. The tot was starting to shoot up and lose his baby fat.

Edmund is nine months older than Charley—how big he must be now! Father, I know you are holding him in your hands, wherever he is, but . . .

Palmer House's Irish housekeeper cleared her throat. "Aye, and 'tis lovely t' be seein' ya home early, Miss Joy."

Joy snapped out of her reverie so quickly that she stammered.

"I-I, um, I happened upon Mr. O'Dell—that is, he was at the cemetery when I-I visited this afternoon."

The rest of her rehearsed statement went straight out of her head, and she blurted, "Mr. O'Dell will be dining with us this evening."

"Oh?" Breona's black eyes gleamed with interest.

Gracie and Olive's joint response was more drawn out.

"Ohhhhh."

They looked at each other, nodded, and tittered.

The Heart of Joy

And every eye in the kitchen fixed upon Joy with increasing speculation.

"*Ja*, and ve vill be happy to see Mr. O'Dell. It has been too long, I think." One side of Marit's mouth twitched as she plopped two more potatoes on the table. "Add these to vat you are peeling. Olive, you vill roll out another pie crust, if you please."

"Yes, Marit," Olive answered.

Joy turned on her heel and shoved through the swinging door, Blackie barely making it through with her before it swung closed.

Alone in the hallway, Joy placed fingers on her face: Her skin was hot to the touch. A scorching, burning red.

"Oh, horse feathers!"

The Palmer House family sat down to dinner at 6:30 each evening. At 6:15, Joy was pacing her cottage at the rear of the house's grounds. She had been dressed for half an hour but was reluctant to go up the back walk to the main house.

Reluctant to find Mr. O'Dell waiting on her.

The Heart of Joy

At 6:25, she could delay no longer.

In her mind, the only thing worse than confronting her dinner guest would be showing up to the dinner table even a minute late—generating yet more undesired attention.

"Whatever in the world possessed me?"

She was fuming as she stomped up the back steps.

Joy entered the dining room from the kitchen to find the residents of Palmer House seated and—as she had feared—every eye fixed on her. A quick glance around the table told her that O'Dell was missing.

Saved! Oh, thank you, Lord!

Oh, but *not* so!

"Joy," Rose said softly. "Your guest is waiting on you in the parlor."

"W-what?"

Rose tilted her head toward the door. "You should hasten. He has been here since six o'clock and you are delaying dinner."

Twenty-one sets of eyes ogled her—and four young ladies giggled behind their hands.

The Heart of Joy

"*Most* unbecoming!" Joy muttered between gritted teeth.

The giggles died out, but the sly grins did not. Old Mr. Wheatley, his sparse hair standing on end, beamed at her—and made no attempt to hide it.

Joy huffed, lifted her chin, and marched out of the dining room, through the great room, across the foyer, and into the parlor. The dark-headed man sitting with his legs crossed stood at once.

"Good evening, Miss Joy," O'Dell said formally.

'Miss Joy'? Not 'Mrs. Michaels'?

Oh, dear.

Joy cleared her throat. Frowned. "Good evening, Mr. O'Dell. I am sorry you have been kept waiting here for me. You could very well have joined the rest of the house at table."

"Ah, yes, of course. However, I did not think it, er, appropriate to present this to you in everyone's presence."

He reached for a tissue-wrapped bundle lying on the little tea table beside the chair. He tendered the bundle to Joy.

The Heart of Joy

Joy stared at the little package with suspicion.

"I-I, um, what is this?"

O'Dell's eyes were merry above his neatly trimmed mustache. "Please feel free to find out."

The muscles in Joy's neck tensed and her tongue, deprived of all saliva, stuck fast to the roof of her mouth. At the same time, she itched to see what the gossamer paper concealed. Ignoring the panicky internal voices urging her to run from the room, Joy folded back the white tissue paper to disclose the gift nestled within.

An orchid corsage, gleaming with moisture, winked at her. The succulent flower's deep purple was edged in ivory.

"Ohhhh!"

"May I pin it on you?"

O'Dell did not wait for an answer. He took the corsage from Joy's stiff, frozen fingers and (quite proficiently) affixed it to the wide lace collar of her dress where the flower's tantalizing scent tickled Joy's nostrils.

"It smells . . . heavenly," Joy gasped. And then she blushed. "But—"

The Heart of Joy

O'Dell cut short the makings of an objection. "Blast! Pardon me, but if we are any later to table, Marit will be serving *our heads* on a platter and not that baked chicken I have been told is on the menu."

He tucked Joy's arm into the crook of his elbow and tugged her along toward the dining room. O'Dell avoided looking at her, but he mentally telegraphed this challenge:

I have fired the first salvo, my dear. Prepare to be wooed until you are won.

A dazed Joy sat on her mother's bed hours later. Dinner had been a stiff, uncomfortable ordeal for her.

Not so for the other diners, including Edmund O'Dell!

No, everyone had enjoyed their dinner and the pleasant table conversation—while Joy's food had tasted more like pasteboard than chicken, and she had been unable to string two words together during the entire meal.

"Mama, I am unsure about starting anything with Mr. O'Dell," Joy explained as best she could. "I still feel married to Grant. I still love him! I do not even know if I believe in love a second time around."

"You forget that I know what it is to love a second time," Rose murmured. "You forget that I still loved my husband, James, even when I married your father. When you were born, I still loved my other children, the children I lost."

"Sometimes I do forget, Mama," Joy admitted.

"I know, too, that your papa still loved your brother Søren's mother, Elli, when he and I realized we were falling in love."

"But . . . but how can you love two men at the same time? How is that possible? How can such a thing be right?"

"When death intervenes and God concludes a marriage, the heart mourns and grieves for what it has lost. It cannot turn off its love like one turns off a spigot. No, the better question concerns the *condition* of the heart: Is it healthy enough to admit that the marriage vows are 'until death do us part' and that death has ended the marriage?

The Heart of Joy

"Can you, Joy, admit that your marriage to Grant is over, even while you hold and esteem every memory as vital and precious— albeit a vital and precious part of your past?"

Joy frowned. *My marriage to Grant is over? But I do not want it to be over!*

She blinked and turned those unwelcome thoughts over and around. "I guess that is where I am at present. I-I do not want to let go of Grant. I want to still be married to him."

"Then, in all fairness, you are not ready to encourage Mr. O'Dell."

But . . .

The thought of letting Grant go had but one rival: Letting O'Dell go, too.

O Lord, I cannot continue on like this, stuck in this lonely place with only my memories of Grant to keep me company!

But am I ready to go forward? Into something new?

And must I let Grant go?

Is that the price I must pay for Edmund O'Dell's love?

The Heart of Joy

The next weeks taxed Joy's soul. That O'Dell was laying siege to her heart was evident.

It is apparent to me and anyone else with two eyes in their head, she fussed.

O'Dell attended the same church the Palmer House residents attended: Calvary Temple, the many-cultured church that met in an old brick warehouse near downtown Denver. Breona's husband, Isaac Carmichael, co-pastored the church with Minister Liáng, who was married to Mei-Xing, a former Palmer House girl.

In the weeks following his dinner at Palmer House, O'Dell had made it a point to greet Rose, Joy, and the other girls (in that order) before each Sunday service. Then he would find a seat directly behind the Palmer House contingency and, after service, linger close by, shamelessly angling for an invitation to Sunday supper.

Breona and Marit were equally shameless in extending such invitations.

Between Sundays, O'Dell called at Palmer House three evenings a week, always after dinner and only

The Heart of Joy

for an hour. When O'Dell arrived, he usually presented Joy with a small gift—nothing too personal, of course. He might bring her a used book of poetry he'd purchased or an article he'd cut from a magazine.

When O'Dell observed Joy's delight over any growing thing he brought, he took to supplying her with little pots of herbs or flowering plants. These arrived singly, a few each week, and with no accompanying fanfare. A little pot simply appeared at Joy's place at the breakfast table.

At first, Joy was not pleased that he called so often. She sometimes asked her mother to tell him that she was busy or unavailable when he asked for her; however, he took no offense.

For the duration of his hour, he played checkers with Mr. Wheatley. To that old gent's delight, Mr. Wheatley and O'Dell played many a game of checkers in May.

Joy pondered the fact that O'Dell seemed undeterred.

Then O'Dell began to call on Saturday afternoons, inviting Joy for a drive. O'Dell made sure to plan their excursion around some interesting scenic viewpoint or historical site. He included Blackie in their outings—and that happy dog, from his place on the Bergdoll's aft seat, hung his head from the open carriage and grinned into the wind.

Quite without intending to, Joy began to look forward to those drives, to anticipate them and wonder what new scenic tour O'Dell would concoct next.

One evening at the end of the month, O'Dell inquired, "Would you care to make a day of Saturday? I thought we could take a lunch and drive to Lookout Mountain Park and hike the trails. No doubt Blackie would find it quite an adventure, and I hear the views are spectacular."

"I would very much like to go!" Joy had heard of the park, too.

She thought for a moment, nodded to herself, and asked softly, "Perhaps you will allow me to put together our lunch?"

Up to that point, O'Dell had made all the arrangements, had borne all the expense of their outings, had accepted that his attentions were one-sided. Joy's suggestion seemed to signal a subtle shift to O'Dell, a restrained concession on Joy's part to receive his courtship.

"I know any lunch you pack will exceed my best efforts," he said. He smiled as he answered, and Joy smiled back.

"It would be advisable for us to wear sturdy walking shoes and be prepared for a mountain shower— extra clothing and a towel or two. Just as a precaution," he added.

"I will dress appropriately," Joy promised.

O'Dell could not take his eyes away. Thirsty for her, he drank in Joy's tall, womanly figure, her high Nordic cheekbones, the striking blue of her eyes, and her flaxen hair—hair so thick that the braid wound and pinned behind her head was as substantial as one of her wrists.

She has her mother's mouth, O'Dell thought. She has Rose's sweet but firm disposition—and all Rose's courage.

Joy blushed under O'Dell's frank examination, but she did not frown as she often had over the past three weeks. She did not fluster and make up a reason to excuse herself.

Perhaps Saturday will be the day, O'Dell thought, *the day I might ask Joy to consider my suit. When we might speak frankly of the future. Our future.*

But how was he to know what misadventures lay ahead?

CHAPTER 3

Saturday morning dawned cloudless and bright, filled with the promise of sunshine and glory. The high mountains would lose the last of their snowpack as spring wound toward summer, but today the snowy peaks to Denver's west still gleamed under the piercing sun.

As soon as they cleared away the breakfast clutter at Palmer House, Joy commandeered the kitchen. She diced a cooked chicken breast, halved grapes, and chopped celery and walnuts. She made sandwiches from the chicken salad and wrapped them in napkins. She filled two large bottles—one with lemonade, the other with water—and corked them.

Joy lined a basket with a tea towel, placed the sandwiches and bottles inside and added two apples, a small cloth and two napkins, and two chipped plates and cups no longer in service but perfect for a picnic.

Marit entered the kitchen with Charley on her hip. "Vat haf you packed for lunch?"

With a sheepish gesture, Joy showed her.

"Ach! Vit so much valking and hiking, Mr. O'Dell vill have more appetite, *ja*? I give cookies and pie, too." She dragged her immense cookie jar toward the basket and piled a dozen oatmeal cookies into yet another napkin. Then she produced a cherry pie, cut two generous slices, placed them on one of the plates, and knotted them into a tea towel. She added two forks to the basket.

"There," she said, satisfied. "That's good, now."

The Heart of Joy

"Thank you, Marit."

"The vay to a man's heart . . ." Marit finished with a chuckle. She grinned and her plain, plump features dimpled and lit with the love and goodwill that made her a favorite at Palmer House.

Joy shook her head and did not trust herself to answer. Instead, she closed the basket and hefted it onto her arm. "Have a good day, sweet Marit."

When the brass knocker fell upon the door and resounded through Palmer House's first floor, Blackie

93

barked and raced to the foyer, skidding across the parquet.

Joy felt within his fluffy ruff for his collar and tugged him back from the door. "Manners, Blackie. Sit."

Obedient to Joy's command, Blackie sat. His tongue lolled out one side of his mouth. He fixed his smoky-blue eyes on the door.

Joy laughed softly. "You know who is calling, do you not, my good boy?"

Blackie whined and scooted his haunches forward an inch.

The Heart of Joy

Joy laughed again and reached for the door. She was still laughing when she greeted O'Dell.

She had never seen him dressed in anything other than one of the three-piece suits he wore as a Pinkerton man. His attire today was a tweed jacket, twill shirt, and a pair of faded trousers over well-used brown boots. Rather than his trademark bowler, he wore a tweed cap upon his head. He held a thick bunch of daisies in his hand.

"A little sunshine for you, Miss Joy." He grinned and extended the bouquet to her.

"Sunshine! What a lovely way to think of flowers! Thank you, Mr. O'Dell."

He eyed her walking dress and boots with approval. "I see you are dressed for our hike."

He approved of more than her attire. Her happy, smiling face caused his heart to swell.

Today, Lord?

"Yes, and I have our lunch and a bag with towels in case of rain."

The Heart of Joy

"I also have a few blankets in the car, should we need them," O'Dell said.

Ten minutes later, they were motoring north and then west toward the snow-topped peaks that crowned the city. Blackie rested his head upon the seat between Joy and O'Dell, and Joy turned sideways to stroke his head.

"How far is Lookout Mountain Park?" she asked.

"I believe it is about twelve miles to the park entrance.

"Depending upon the road and terrain, it should take about an hour to reach it. One of my men tells me that the road winds up the mountain from the entrance and has a number of hiking trails and overlooks along the way. He mentioned Wildcat Point as particularly impressive."

"Blackie will love it all."

"Did you bring a leash for him?"

"Oh, yes. I do not fear that he would run off, but he might dash into a hedge of brambles or surprise a skunk. I would not relish spending the evening combing

The Heart of Joy

stickers from his coat—and I cannot bear to speak of the other."

"No, indeed."

The dirt road of the Lariat Trail turned back on itself many times as they crawled toward the park's entrance and beyond. Soon the scrubby brush gave way to a sprinkling of Ponderosa pines and they spied hiking trails leading away from the track, deeper into the trees.

O'Dell pulled his auto to the edge of the road. "Shall we hike up those rocks to the overlook and see what we might see? Then perhaps we could take our lunch and hike higher—up that trail."

"Yes. That sounds good."

Joy fastened Blackie's leash to his collar before she got out. He whined and pushed at the rear door, anxious to explore.

They climbed a hill of rocks to the vantage point, O'Dell ahead of Joy. At one particularly high step, he turned and offered his hand.

"Good heavens. Women's skirts are so confining! It is a wonder you can lift your foot high enough."

Without hesitation or fore-thought, Joy placed her hand in his, and he pulled her up. They arrived at the overlook a moment later and gazed in awe at the wide plain below them. Denver was miniscule from their high viewpoint, and they stood in silence to admire it.

O'Dell had not released Joy's hand, and Joy was conscious of the sensation of her bare hand in his.

It feels . . . nice, she admitted.

O'Dell's private reflections were a bit more enthusiastic.

O Lord, how I long to draw this woman to me! It would take but a tug of my hand to pull her into my arms . . .

His behavior was, however, more sensible than his enthusiasm.

After pointing out all the landmarks they could recognize and name—and in answer to Blackie's insistence that they continue to explore—they clambered back down the rocks. As it turned out, Joy required more assistance climbing down than climbing up, several boulders being harder to navigate in a lady-like manner.

O'Dell took Blackie's leash from Joy and held her hand, glad to render his assistance.

The Heart of Joy

Then they plucked the basket from O'Dell's auto and approached a trail that ran uphill into the trees.

"I brought this for you should the trail get steep." O'Dell pulled a walking stick from the car and brandished it. "I will carry it until you should find that you need it."

He shouldered the basket, and Joy, with a firm hold on Blackie's leash, took the lead a few yards ahead of O'Dell. Blackie, eager to explore, pulled her onward.

Before long, they reached the top of the slope, and the trail continued through the trees on more level ground. Joy enjoyed the soft light filtering through the green boughs; the spring breeze was just enough to cool her from her exertions.

Joy breathed a contented sigh. *What a perfect day!*

The trail before them bent sharply to the right. Perhaps a few yards before they reached the bend, another dog trotted into view. He was a bull of an animal—a full-grown black and tan Rottweiler,

The Heart of Joy

thick in body, topped by an
enormous head and jowls.

The dog no sooner glimpsed
Blackie than he snarled and
charged.

"Joy!" O'Dell dropped the
basket and raced toward her.

Blackie, sensing the danger,
stopped where he was, but the other
dog was on him in an instant—
snapping, biting, tearing, dragging
the smaller dog to the ground.

Joy shrieked and let go of the
leash and was about to plunge into
the fight when O'Dell's hand jerked
her back.

He swung the walking stick at the attacking dog's head. Again and again, he struck it, but his blows made little difference. The Rottweiler's ferocious growls and Blackie's piteous cries filled the air.

Joy's screams added to the horror. "Edmund! Edmund! He is killing Blackie! Help him!"

O'Dell straddled the huge animal, reached both hands around its head and, with immense effort, pulled him off Blackie.

At once, the beast rounded on O'Dell and sank his bared teeth into O'Dell's left forearm. Shaking his heavy head, he ripped through O'Dell's jacket and into his arm. O'Dell kicked at the brute, landing blow after blow on its chest, but the dog's jaws only clamped down harder and shook O'Dell, tearing more deeply into skin and muscle.

Joy's screams and the sounds of the attack summoned the other dog's owner. He ran toward the melee—in time to see O'Dell pull his snub-nosed revolver from the shoulder holster under his jacket.

"No!"

But O'Dell fired point-blank into the Rottweiler's head. The animal's jaws released, and his body dropped to the dirt.

The dog's owner cursed O'Dell. "Ya killed him! Ya killed m' Brutus! Ya din't need t' kill him!"

The man called down many and varied curses on O'Dell's head, but O'Dell spared him no attention. His arm hung limp from the shredded tatters of his jacket. It streamed blood. He whipped a kerchief from his back pocket and tried to staunch the flow. It was not enough, not even close.

The dog's owner continued to curse O'Dell.

The Heart of Joy

"You are an irresponsible fool," O'Dell told the man. "Where were you? Your dog attacked us without provocation. I will have you brought up on charges!"

The man ignored him and mourned over his dead dog's body.

After the cacophony of the attack, Joy's screams, his shouts, and the gunshot, O'Dell realized the forest world was strangely silent. With his arm still bleeding liberally, he turned around.

Joy sat in the dust of the trail, Blackie's lifeless body in her lap. She cradled him and rocked forward and back, keening without making a sound.

"Oh, no," O'Dell whispered. "Oh, no."

He knelt in front of Joy. Blood splattered her cheek and smeared her chin. The white of Blackie's ruff was stained an ugly red; his throat had been savaged.

His soft blue eyes were blank. Empty.

With his good hand, O'Dell touched Joy's shoulder. "Oh, Joy! I'm so terribly sorry."

Joy's eyes, as blank and empty as Blackie's, gazed at nothing.

CHAPTER 4

Joy's screams and the gunfire had drawn two young gentlemen who were also hiking the trail. They took stock of the situation and straight away offered their services. One of the men bound up O'Dell's arm with napkins from the lunch basket. At O'Dell's request, the other returned to O'Dell's automobile and brought back a blanket.

Joy watched, silent and unresponsive, as one of the men and O'Dell, despite his discomfort, laid out the blanket, placed Blackie's body on it, and folded the blanket about him.

O'Dell was weak, though. Blood ran from his makeshift bandages and dripped to the ground. Shock and blood loss were taking their toll.

"You need a doctor," one of the two men observed. "Would you like me to drive you and your lady back to town? My cousin will follow behind in our auto."

"Yes, thank you." O'Dell stood up and had to lean upon a tree to steady himself. "And that man. He must come with us to answer for his dog's actions."

The Rottweiler's owner, still belligerent, bellowed at O'Dell. "Ya killed m' dog. Ya ain't got no right t' tell me what t' do!"

O'Dell reached into his trouser pocket and retrieved his Pinkerton badge. "I am executing a citizen's arrest on charges of reckless endangerment." He shoved his badge into his pocket and again pulled his revolver from its holster.

Perhaps it was the shock of his injury, perhaps his outrage over Blackie's unjust demise. Some of the old O'Dell surfaced in the cold threat he growled. "You will come along peaceably, or I will shoot you where you stand."

Nathan and Peter, the cousins who had come to their aid, tried their best to stem the flow from O'Dell's arm. They employed the towels from O'Dell's auto and again bandaged his arm, but in spite of their efforts, fresh, red blood seeped from their improvised dressings and ran down O'Dell's trousers.

The Heart of Joy

"Best to get you down the mountain," Nathan said. "We will drive you."

Peter retrieved his auto and the two vehicles returned to Denver.

O'Dell did not recall much after that. He rode in Peter's automobile with his gun trained on the dead dog's defiant owner; however, he struggled to remain conscious during the drive. Nathan followed them in O'Dell's auto. Joy sat in the rear seat with Blackie's wrapped body close to her side.

Their first stop, at O'Dell's insistence, was the U.S. Marshal's office. His old friend, Marshal Pounder, took the Rottweiler's owner into custody.

Pounder agreed that the marshals had jurisdiction. "It happened outside of Denver city limits. We'll hold him."

He eyed O'Dell. "I'd say you look like a ghost, Ed, but you're a mite too green. Better get to a doctor pronto."

"No. I must take Joy home first." O'Dell's words were slurred, but he was resolute.

"Right you are. D'ya trust me to do that for you?"

The Heart of Joy

O'Dell blinked in slow motion, stupid from shock and blood loss.

"I'll see to Mrs. Michaels. Your friends here will take you to the doc's."

O'Dell acquiesced with one jerky nod of his head.

"Marshal, if you please, I choose to accompany Mr. O'Dell."

Joy stood in the doorway of Pounder's office. Her hair was a disheveled mess, her dress sullied and blood-soaked. The first horror of Blackie's death had worn off.

"As you wish, ma'am."

Marshal Pounder thanked Nathan and Pete, and the two good Samaritans went on their way.

Pounder then telephoned Palmer House and gave Rose the short version of the events. The marshal and Joy trundled O'Dell into his car and, following Joy's directions, Pounder drove them to the offices of Palmer House's physician, Doctor Murphy.

O'Dell was as pale as death when they arrived. Dr. Murphy's assistant and Pounder more or less carried O'Dell into the doctor's office.

The Heart of Joy

"Take him straight back to the surgery," Doctor Murphy instructed. He and his nurse followed Pounder and the orderly through to the surgery and began organizing the supplies and instruments he would need.

The doctor looked up when Joy entered. "No, Mrs. Michaels. This is no place for you. Please wait in the reception area."

His nurse scooted Joy out of the surgery and closed the door behind her, leaving Joy blinking at the door's unyielding panels.

"But . . ." Joy did not know how to speak, how to articulate what she felt.

But I belong with him.

Sometime later, the door to the doctor's offices opened. Rose entered followed by Breona.

Joy fell into her mother's embrace. "Mama. Breona. Thank you for coming." She was glad to see them but too emotionally spent to express anything other than muted relief.

The Heart of Joy

She looked from Breona to Rose. "H-how did you get here?"

"Pastor Carmichael. Breona called him, and he brought us. He should be in directly."

"How ist Mr. O'Dell?" Breona asked.

"I do not know. They would not allow me to stay with him."

Rose nodded, looked around the waiting room. "And where have you left Blackie?"

Joy began to shake and weep. "Oh, Mama—he is dead. Blackie is dead! The other dog killed him!"

"Oh, my darling, my Joy!" Rose wept with her daughter and held her close. Breona, tears glimmering in her own eyes, placed her arms around Rose and Joy.

Breona's husband, Isaac Carmichael, found them that way.

Soon after Joy's tears had subsided, Marshal Pounder slipped into the room, and Joy looked to him with expectation.

"How is Mr. O'Dell?"

"The doctor is stitching up his wounds." Pounder breathed a little laugh. "He sent me out, too, as I was not necessary. I may be a

The Heart of Joy

lawman, but frankly, the sight of so much—"

He caught himself and cleared his throat. "I beg your pardon, ladies, for speaking indelicately."

Joy nodded. "There is no need to apologize. I thank you for your assistance today, Marshal. We are most grateful."

❧ ✹ ☙

Yet even later, the doctor himself came out. "I have finished what I can do for Mr. O'Dell. The superficial wounds were easy enough to stitch up. He has, however, sustained some deeper, more serious injuries to muscle and nerve. I will not know if he will suffer permanent damage to his arm until everything heals."

He looked from Rose to Joy and included Pounder. "He is going to be weak from loss of blood and in great pain. He will require nursing for a few days until he regains some strength. If you cannot accommodate his needs, I will place him in the hospital."

"We will take him," Rose answered.

"Yes," Joy agreed.

The Heart of Joy

"Very good. Bring him back first thing in the morning. I will change the dressing on his wounds and show one of you how to do the same. Someone must care for his wounds and keep them clean for the next several weeks. We do not know the health of the dog that bit him, so the greatest precautions are necessary to prevent infection."

Joy looked to Marshal Pounder. "We will ride home with Pastor Carmichael. Would you be so good as to drive Mr. O'Dell's automobile and follow us to Palmer House? I am certain Pastor Carmichael will then return you to your office."

The door to the surgery opened again, and O'Dell appeared, supported by the nurse and orderly. O'Dell was conscious, but barely so. His forearm, bound in layers of gauze and bandaging, was twice its normal size.

Doctor Murphy followed and handed Rose a sheet of paper. "Follow these instructions, please, the most important of which is to telephone me immediately should his wounds soak through the bandages—copious amounts of

The Heart of Joy

blood would signal a bleeding vessel. You may see some staining, but you should not see a great deal of fresh blood. And I have painted the wounds with iodine to prevent sepsis. A dog bite can be quite problematic. Call me also if he becomes feverish."

He handed Rose a brown bottle. "One teaspoon for pain every three hours whether he feels he needs it or not. I wish for you to keep ahead of his pain rather than behind."

"Thank you, Doctor," Rose murmured.

"I will see you in the morning," Doctor Murphy told O'Dell.

O'Dell moved his head side to side in slow motion. "Not sure . . . how I'll manage that."

"Your friends will be caring for you until you are a bit farther down the road to recovery," Murphy told him.

"They will?" O'Dell was too dazed to put it all together.

"Come along, O'Dell." Pounder motioned to Isaac Carmichael and the two men took over from the nurse and orderly. They assisted their friend from the office and into

the back seat of Pastor
Carmichael's vehicle. Breona took
the front seat next to her husband.
Rose climbed in on one side of
O'Dell, Joy on the other, to keep
their patient upright.

Pounder followed them in
O'Dell's automobile. The ride to
Palmer House did not take more
than a quarter of an hour, during
which time O'Dell's chin nodded on
his chest and he occasionally
groaned when the vehicle ran over
a rough patch of road.

At Rose's direction, Breona and Joy made up a bed for O'Dell in Palmer House's library. Marshal Pounder, aided by Isaac Carmichael, steered an unsteady O'Dell into the room and got him undressed and under the covers. Pastor Carmichael administered a dose from the brown bottle Rose had handed him.

"Whole lotta fuss over a small dog bite," O'Dell grumbled.

"There was nothing small about the dog or the bite, from what I hear," Isaac replied. "And you are weak as rainwater from loss of blood."

The Heart of Joy

The only response Pastor Carmichael and Marshal Pounder received was the sound of deep, even breathing.

"Out like a candle," Pounder noted as they crept away. They joined Joy and Rose in the great room.

"Someone will need to fetch a few items from Mr. O'Dell's rooms," Rose said. "Several nightshirts, socks, razor. A change of clothes."

Pounder was the first to volunteer. "I'd be happy to go for you, Miss Rose, but I'd feel better if you or Miss Joy rifled through his things to get what you think is needed."

"I'll go with you."

Joy surprised herself by how quickly she volunteered.

O'Dell's two rooms, a simple bedroom and sitting room in a modest boarding house, provided an intriguing glimpse into the man's private life, but that glimpse was a disappointment to Joy.

She studied the sitting room, noting the threadbare furnishings and lack of personalization. Only the Bible and a stack of books on the table by his easy chair piqued her interest or told her anything about O'Dell's private, everyday life. His bedroom, while tidy, was no more revealing.

Everything seems so . . . impersonal. Temporary. And a bit impoverished.

While Pounder looked on, Joy located O'Dell's toiletries. She selected three clean nightshirts and two changes of clothes and placed them in a carpetbag she found at the top of his wardrobe. She added his Bible atop the clothing and toiletries. Before she told Pounder that she was finished, she glanced around the apartment again.

I suppose I believed Mr. O'Dell to be more prosperous, Joy admitted to herself. *As chief of the Denver Pinkerton office, I assumed his living quarters would have a bit more . . . substance. His personal dress contradicts the sparseness of these rooms.*

Joy's thoughts wandered down a dark path. *Is Mr. O'Dell a spendthrift? Or a secret gambler? Could he be indebted?*

The Heart of Joy

Almost as quickly, she rejected those accusations. *No, I cannot believe any of those things of him.*

What she did not allow herself to voice inwardly kept creeping and pushing into her thoughts anyway: *I assumed he would be able to take a wife. Appearances seem to indicate that I was wrong.*

Joy handed off the carpetbag to her mother as Marshal Pounder and Pastor Carmichael said their goodbyes. Marshal Pounder would leave O'Dell's automobile at Palmer

House and ride back to his office with Pastor Carmichael.

"Miz Michaels?" Mr. Wheatley, deferential and apologetic, waited for a private word with Joy. The grizzled old man looked as weary as Joy felt.

"Yes, Mr. Wheatley?"

"Would you, that is, shall I . . . shall I dig a little place in the rose garden for Blackie?"

Over the last chaotic hours, Joy had been distracted from the horror of Blackie's demise. It crashed upon her afresh at Mr. Wheatley's soft query.

The Heart of Joy

"Ohhh . . ."

Faintness swept over her.

"Here, miss. Sit down now for a minute." Mr. Wheatley helped her onto a sofa.

Rose rushed to her side. "What is it?"

Joy shook her head, too overcome to answer.

"It was me. I-I asked if I should . . . prepare a place for good ol' Blackie in the rose garden." Mr. Wheatley's countenance was downcast. As defeated as Joy's.

"Oh, my darling! In the commotion surrounding Mr. O'Dell's

wounds and getting him settled, I confess I had, for the moment, forgotten about dear Blackie."

Joy swallowed and ground the heels of her hands into her eyes in an attempt to curb her tears. "I had, too."

"Are you able to give Mr. Wheatley an answer?"

"Yes, of course." Joy lifted her face. "The rose garden would be perfect, dear friend. Thank you."

Mr. Wheatley nodded. "I am honored to do this last service for him."

The Heart of Joy

When he had shuffled from the room, Rose sat beside Joy and took her hand. "If you are able, will you tell me what happened?"

"Oh, Mama. It started as such a lovely day, a perfect day. The weather was beautiful. We stopped at an overlook and saw all of Denver spread below us. The view was all we had hoped for.

"Afterwards, we chose to hike a trail into the trees. Blackie was on his leash, of course, and was so eager to explore. He and I were a bit ahead of Mr. O'Dell on the trail. We had not gone far when a giant of a dog rounded the curve before us. He s-saw Blackie, and-and h-he attacked."

Joy sobbed. "Oh, Mama! I cannot rid myself of the sight and sound of that brute tearing into Blackie, snapping at his throat. My poor boy! How he cried! He was no match for the other dog, no match at all.

"When that beast charged Blackie, of course I tried to throw myself into the fray and save him. Mr. O'Dell held me back. He beat the other dog with his walking stick, but it was as though the monster had no sensitivities, as if he could not feel the beating.

"When Mr. O'Dell saw that his efforts were in vain, he straddled the dog as one mounts a horse. He put his arms about the dog's throat and pulled him from Blackie. That is when the dog turned on him. He sank his teeth into Mr. O'Dell's arm with the same ferocity as he had ravaged poor Blackie."

"But how in the world did Mr. O'Dell escape him?"

"I was not aware that Mr. O'Dell carries a gun at all times. He reached within his jacket and brought it out. He fired it into the monster's head."

"Oh! Oh, my dear!" Joy's narrative conjured images that stunned Rose.

"I ran to Blackie, of course. That awful dog had mauled Blackie so badly that my poor boy could not even whine. He just stared at me, as though begging me to help him. I sat in the dirt and pulled him onto my lap. He-he licked my hand, just once. And then he was gone. I saw the moment the light faded from his sweet eyes.

The Heart of Joy

"Mama! Blackie is gone! Oh, Jesus, please help me!"

Rose tugged Joy to her, and Joy buried her face in Rose's lap as she had done as a child. She wept and grieved for the loss of her companion, but also for the loss of her last tie to Grant.

She cried for some time. When the storm eased and passed, Joy sat up and wiped her eyes. Rose rubbed her daughter's back as Joy composed herself.

"I am quite grateful for one thing in this tragic day, Joy, one thing very near to my heart," Rose whispered.

Joy was distracted, but she asked, "What is that, Mama?"

"I am grateful for Mr. O'Dell. Even though he was seriously injured, my mind cannot help but wonder what might have happened to you had he not been there, had he not prevented you from trying to save Blackie."

Joy stared at the carpet. "I would have been savaged, just as Blackie was. And I-I could not have prevailed. There is no knowing how I would have fared."

The Heart of Joy

"Mr. O'Dell saved you, my daughter," Rose whispered. "I know how precious Blackie was to you . . . but *you*, Joy, are my only surviving child. I owe Mr. O'Dell a great debt."

Joy sniffled and turned over her mother's words. After a moment, a frown drew her brows together.

"Mama, do you not find it . . . difficult to understand, hard to fathom, how everything dear to me is always taken away?"

While Rose tried to frame an answer, Joy sighed. "Perhaps I was mistaken to encourage Mr. O'Dell, to even consider encouraging him. I lose those whom I love. He could be the next to be taken."

"No, Joy. That is most certainly wrong thinking," Rose protested.

"Why is it wrong, Mama? Do I wish something ill to befall Mr. O'Dell? No, I do not." She shook her head. "I must break with him, the sooner the better. I-I could not bear it if—"

Joy's spine stiffened with resolve. "Please do not ask me to assist in Mr. O'Dell's care, Mama. I must not embolden him further."

CHAPTER 5

"If Tabitha were here instead of at nursing school in Boulder, you would be receiving quality care, Mr. O'Dell, rather than my poor ministrations." Rose finished changing the bandages on O'Dell's arm. "I apologize for our less-than-professional attention these past three days."

"Not at all. Doctor Murphy is pleased with my progress. Marit has fed me like a king, you and Breona have kept my wounds dressed, and Mr. Wheatley has seen to my personal needs and honed my skill at checkers. What more could I ask for?"

Rose smiled and her gray eyes watched him. "Perhaps a little more appreciation from my daughter?"

O'Dell flushed. He wanted to avoid Rose's attempt to steer their conversation toward Joy, but the note he'd received from Joy burned with cold fire under the pillow of his makeshift bed in the library. He had read the unexpected and painful missive so many times that he had committed it to memory.

The Heart of Joy

Dear Mr. O'Dell,

The tragic event that wounded you has prompted me to think upon our friendship with fresh light. I confess that I was weak in spirit and mistaken to allow your suit to progress. I see more clearly now and have arrived at the settled conclusion that we must not pursue a deeper friendship than that which we have enjoyed these last years.

I thank you for your care and for your every effort to locate my son. I owe you a continuing debt of gratitude.

I ask you, please, to respect my wishes in this.

Sincerely,

Joy Michaels

O'Dell chose to be frank with Rose. "Joy has asked me not to court her."

Sorrow swirled in Rose's soft gray eyes. "She said this to you?"

"She wrote it."

"I see."

O'Dell snorted. "I do not see. What is she so afraid of?"

Rose touched O'Dell's hand. "You are correct, dear Edmund.

The Heart of Joy

Fear is the problem. She is afraid. Afraid she will lose yet another soul she has grown to love."

The few words Rose spoke were laden with so many revelations that O'Dell's head spun.

Joy's mother addressed me by my Christian name? What does that imply?

Joy is afraid? What does she fear?

Wait.

Joy has grown to love me?

Only one question made it to his mouth. "She loves me?"

"I believe she does."

"But?"

"But Blackie's death and your injury have made her, again, more aware of how fragile life is. Think on it: She lost her father, her husband, and her son in less than two years' time. She is afraid to hope for happiness. She is frightened that something will befall you and she will, again, be left alone."

He stared, his brows drawn down, at the pattern in the carpet.

"I can attest that you are a gentleman, Edmund, and I believe you would honor Joy's request despite the pain it would cause you. However, that does not mean I believe her decision is the right one or that you should give up your suit entirely."

"No? What else is there to do? She asked me to respect her wishes. I will not bully her. Not ever."

"What else is there to do, Edmund? Why, we should do what God commands us to do when confronted with difficulties, even impossibilities. We should pray. *You* should pray, Edmund. Do you believe our great God wishes you and Joy to marry? Then you should ask wisdom of the Lord, who is gracious to all who approach him, and he will direct your steps."

O'Dell held his injured arm and pondered Rose's advice.

Yes, I should pray, he thought. *Perhaps the Lord will show me how to break down the wall of fear in Joy's heart.*

"I believe I should go home today," he told Rose. "Although it will take some time before my arm is fully functional, I must get back to my work."

The Heart of Joy

He snorted a little laugh. "My only difficulty will be dressing the wounds with one hand."

Rose nodded. "If you would care to stop by each morning, I would be happy to see to your dressings for you."

"You have been most kind to me, Mrs. Thoresen."

"No, Edmund, you have been kind to us, to me, in particular. I wish to thank you for protecting my daughter—my only surviving child—from the animal that mauled you. I know you would have saved Blackie, too, if you could have."

She took his good hand in hers. "Will you call me Rose, Edmund?"

He stared into her face, seeing there the acceptance he sought from Joy. "You approve of my suit?"

"Yes, with all my heart. And I beg of you not to give up hope, despite the letter Joy has written to you. I know she has feelings for you."

"I had hoped she had."

"Do seek the Lord—and be patient a little longer? She is still sorting things out."

The Heart of Joy

"He has gone home?" Joy had spent so much energy avoiding O'Dell that she found herself nonplussed at Rose's matter-of-fact announcement.

"Yes. Dr. Murphy believes the danger of infection to be past, and Mr. O'Dell feels he can manage on his own. He will come each morning for me to change the dressings."

Rose studied Joy for a moment. Her daughter's expression was a mixture of relief and disappoint- ment, resolve and longing.

"Have you given up Mr. O'Dell, then, Joy?"

Joy's chin dropped. "I-I, yes. I have."

"And you have done so because you fear for him?"

Joy frowned. "I suppose that is one way of looking at it."

"So you, a child of The Most High God, now take your guidance from your fears? Has God instructed us to live in fear, to give fear a place in our lives, to be led by our fears?"

Joy shifted on her feet, disturbed by the direction of the conversation. "Well, no, of course not, but—"

The Heart of Joy

"No 'buts,' Joy. Is fear from God or of God? Is confusion? What does Scripture tell us? Are we to be ordered, counseled, or guided by our fears?"

"No."

"Exactly. *No*. We are, rather, commanded *not* to fear—that is, not to allow fear to rule us. We are to obey God, even in the face of our fears. I suggest that you pray past your fears, Joy—past their hold upon you.

"I would add that if you aspire to live a life free from the risk of loss, then you will be lonely and fearful all your days. Life is fraught with risk. As Christians, we are not to live our lives doing all we can to avoid the possibility of heartache. We are to face our fears and stand strong in the love and hope of God."

Rose reached out and lifted Joy's chin. "And I think you should consider something else, my dear daughter. I think you should stop and imagine your life without Mr. O'Dell. Consider what it will be like if you turn down Mr. O'Dell and he goes away, never to return. Just for a moment, think of your life without him, a future in which he does not figure."

Joy did not want to. She knew she could not bear to look there—for a vast, gaping void stretched out before her—an aching empty-ness that had nothing to do with her love for Grant or his absence.

Something inside of her clenched at the idea of never seeing O'Dell again, and she could not answer her mother.

"Edmund O'Dell loves you, Joy. You have a long life still ahead of you, so I must bring to your remembrance something else."

Joy licked her lips and whispered, "What is it, Mama?"

"Your father's last words to you."

Rose did not need to rehearse them to Joy. Her father's words were burned upon Joy's heart, and she could hear his voice as he struggled to pronounce his dying blessing upon her.

In her mind's eye, Joy saw her papa's figure under the covers, so still, so much smaller than was right, not at all like the man upon whose shoulders she had ridden as a child. Joy had sat on a chair

The Heart of Joy

beside her father's deathbed and held his hand in her own.

"Papa? Papa, it's Joy. I'm here, Papa!" she had called to him.

She had felt a gentle pressure and, as she lifted her face, had seen his eyes searching for her. She had stood and leaned over so he could see her.

"Here I am, Papa."

"My . . . my Joy Again."

Rose and Jan had named her "Joy Again." She was their joy after sorrow, their happiness after so much loss.

In her memory, Joy called out to her father. *"Yes, Papa!"*

"Joy, my Joy . . . I b-bless . . . I bless you and . . . your chil . . . dren . . . my daugh . . . ter."

He had struggled to take another breath.

"Your chil . . . dren. The Lord will . . . give you."

Jan had blessed his daughter, her and *her children*. And yet, through the years of her marriage to Grant, Joy had been childless, unable to conceive. At the time of Jan's death, Joy had been living in Corinth, not far from Denver. The

The Heart of Joy

year prior, Grant's ship had gone
down in the Atlantic, with all hands
lost, and Joy was living as a widow.

*I could not give credence to
Papa's blessing when I heard it*, Joy
thought. *I had no husband, and
God had not blessed us with
children.*

But then—oh! such great
rejoicing! Grant had returned from
a watery grave. His memories had
been seared by fever and one arm
made useless from floating in the
sea while tangled in a life preserver.
But he had returned to Joy.

Not long afterwards, Joy had become pregnant with baby Edmund. During her pregnancy, Joy had turned Jan's blessing over in her heart and begun to believe that more children were coming.

Until Edmund was taken.

Until Grant's damaged heart gave out.

"Joy?"

"Yes, Mama." Joy's answer was automatic.

"God is not bound by time, place, or circumstance as we are. His promises are sure."

The Heart of Joy

Joy blinked and allowed Rose's words to tumble about in her mind.

O'Dell stared around his plain, sparsely furnished rooms, the conversation with Rose Thoresen fresh in his mind.

"What else is there to do, Edmund? Why, we should do what God commands us to do when confronted with difficulties, even impossibilities. We should pray. You should pray, Edmund. Do you believe our great God wishes you and Joy to marry? Then you should ask wisdom of the Lord, who is

gracious to all who approach him, and he will direct your steps."

He dropped to his knees in front of a chair and bent his head. "Lord," he whispered, "you know my heart. You know that I desire Joy, that I wish to marry her. I cannot believe that the love I have for her is wrong, that you do not bless my feelings for her, because she has made me a better man, Lord. It was the testimony of her life that first pricked at my hard heart and made me reconsider my godless state.

The Heart of Joy

"But you also know what is best for me—and for her. If Joy is not your plan for me, I am willing, Lord God, to follow your direction for my life. And if I am not your plan for her life . . . well, Lord, I desire only your best for her. I care more for her spiritual and eternal condition than my own selfish, temporal happiness.

"So, if I am to put her aside, if that is your will, I submit to it. Please speak to me, so that I will know your direction."

His voice rasped. "But if your plan for me includes Joy, will you show me what I am to do?"

The recent memory of Joy, sitting in the dust and dirt of the hiking trail, intruded. She was weeping and hugging Blackie's body to herself, her dress smeared with Blackie's lifeblood.

O'Dell shook his head. *How she loved that dog and will grieve for him.*

His wounded arm began to itch. He cradled the arm on his lap and resisted the temptation to rub or scratch the itch that tickled and tingled within the swaddling of bandages. But the more he resisted, the more it begged to be scratched.

His thoughts wandered back several years, to the six months he had spent in Corinth posing as a British gentleman of ease. In this guise, O'Dell had arrived in the mountains above Denver, supposedly for hunting sport. In reality, he had been the Pinkerton Agency's crack Missing Persons Investigator—and he had come to Colorado to locate and retrieve a number of women missing from back east.

His hunt for the predators who betrayed the trust of innocent girls and women had landed him in Corinth. Quite by chance, he had taken a room at Corinth Mountain Lodge—the lodge Joy owned. When O'Dell and Joy had discovered that their missions intersected, they joined forces to put an end to the traffickers and their schemes.

In absentminded response, he rubbed at the spot on his arm that itched. It did no good. In fact, the itching began to travel.

The Heart of Joy

"Confound it!" he muttered. He tugged his thoughts away from the aggravating tickle, back to Corinth, where something different niggled in his mind.

He was standing outside the tiny Corinth grocery store—but he was not alone. Joy was on his arm—Joy, the widowed Mrs. Michaels, for Grant was still presumed dead. They stepped into the shop. A box of puppies whined and fussed behind the grocer's counter.

"My Bessie gave me a new litter of pups a few weeks back," the

grocer informed them. "Would you like to see?"

Joy crossed behind the counter and looked under it. In a wooden crate, a black dog with a single white patch at her throat nursed six chubby puppies.

"Pick one up if you like," Mr. Marsh said.

She stooped, and when she stood, she was holding a black ball of curling fur.

"Aren't you beautiful?" Joy had crooned.

O'Dell had known at that exact moment that he loved Joy.

The Heart of Joy

Stifling an oath, he jumped to his feet and paced while, as much as he could bear, he rubbed the flat of his palm across the itching and tingling of his many stitches.

He was certain his arm was on fire.

The picture of Joy with the puppy snuggled at her neck persisted. As he stared into it, weeks flew by in his memory.

Then . . .

He was sitting within the lodge's pantry, a slatted wood box at his feet. The box trembled and emitted a quivering little whine. It had gone against his grain to let the puppy cry, but O'Dell had wanted—had needed—for Joy to hear the puppy's whimpers and come to investigate.

And she had.

She had thrown open the pantry door and taken in the strange scene: O'Dell lounging upon a straight-back chair beside a box containing a few odd rags . . . and a pudgy, black pup with a white ruff.

He had tipped his derby down over one eye and drawled, "I've been sitting here ever so long . . .

The Heart of Joy

I believe the little guy is getting hungry. And the fact is, I detest dog hair."

He had added in a dry tone, "Particularly on this suit."

"I don't understand."

"I was remiss," he'd replied.

"I beg your pardon?"

"Not at all—I am asking your pardon. I completely neglected to give you your Christmas gift."

"My what?" Joy had stared at the whimpering puppy with unveiled longing.

O'Dell had stood and flicked an imaginary speck of lint from his sleeve. "Merry Christmas . . . albeit two months late."

O'Dell stopped scratching at his arm. "Why . . . why, that's it."

He grabbed for his hat and raced from the room.

I thank you, Father, for answered prayer.

"Now, Lord, if you will direct me where to look . . ."

CHAPTER 6

The final battle of O'Dell's war to win Joy's heart commenced a week later.

It had been ten days since Joy had written the note to O'Dell. During the ten days following, Joy's moods had alternated between defensive and morose, had vacillated between short-tempered and weepy. On any given day or at any moment, the collective souls residing under Palmer House's roof could never guess which Joy to expect—nor could they anticipate her reaction to the box she found sitting on her chair at breakfast that morning.

And since they could not prepare for that which they could not anticipate, the residents of Palmer House awaited Joy's arrival at breakfast with some trepidation.

Joy eyed the box on her chair.

"What is this?" she demanded through pursed lips.

Rose, who continued to butter her toast, murmured, "It is addressed to you, so I am certain we cannot tell you."

The Heart of Joy

Joy sniffed. "Well, from where did it come?" Her frown signaled suspicion. Distrust.

"I believe Mr. O'Dell delivered it this morning."

Joy heaved a sigh. A long, dreary day loomed before her, and she did not appreciate the drama with which it was beginning.

Is this not so like Edmund O'Dell? she fumed within herself. *I should have known he would disregard my wishes. Now, if I hope to have my breakfast before catching the trolley to my shop, I must take precious time to dispose of this box and its contents—while everyone here enjoys a good laugh at my expense.*

Joy glared around the table, but no one met her accusing gaze. Billy, Marit, and Rose managed to keep their faces toward their plates.

Well! Mama must have cautioned one and all to mind their own business—the girls in particular. They are so everlastingly nosy!

Indeed, the girls said nothing as they slanted their eyes anywhere but in Joy's direction.

The Heart of Joy

That is, they *said* nothing, but they frowned, they sighed, they grimaced, they bit their tongues, and they squirmed in their seats—but they managed (at least verbally) to curb their burning curiosity.

Mr. Wheatley, however, seemed under no such restriction. And so, while his companions at table were mute, he beamed in Joy's direction and pronounced, "You sure do get a lot of pretties from that Mr. O'Dell. Mighty nice young feller, he is. Good checker player, too. Say, you going to open your present?"

His last word snagged six-year-old Will's attention. "Who got a present? Can I see? Are you going to open it? Please?"

And that, of course, set off his little brother Charley. "Present! Present!" he hollered, clapping his hands at the same time.

Joy tossed her head. "I most certainly will not open this-this-this—*whatever* it is. The table is neither the appropriate time nor place."

Her announcement drew an immediate and universal growl of

dissatisfaction from the breakfast crowd.

"Aw, nuts!" Will flounced back in his chair and pouted.

His father frowned and chastised him. "Why, William Evans! You will mind your manners, young man."

Uncertain about what was happening—but certain about gifts of any kind, Charley pounded his spoon on the table with enthusiasm. "I wanna present! I wanna present! Present! Present!"

"She ain't gonna open her stupid old present, Charley," Will grumbled. He glanced at his dad and lapsed into sullen silence, but he cut his eyes toward Joy.

The scowl Will slanted toward Joy disconcerted her. At the same moment, she caught Olive crossing her eyes and sticking out her tongue in Joy's general direction.

Joy's face reddened, and she exploded. "Fine! That is the *last straw*. I will neither entertain nor reward such a lapse in manners and common civility. Directly into the trash it goes."

She swept the box from her chair and into her arms—and

stopped cold when the box's contents shifted.

Skidded.

Thudded.

Whined.

"No . . ." Joy plopped, rather than sat, into her chair with the box on her lap. She swallowed hard before she prized open the box's flaps and stared at the ball of fur cowering in one corner.

The black-and-white puppy was, perhaps, too young to be separated from her mother. She shivered and quaked and uttered a piteous whimper.

The raw, hard, fearful spot in Joy's heart melted. With tears shimmering on her lashes, she scooped up the tiny bundle and clasped it to her breast. The puppy quivered and yipped.

"Shhhhh, little one," Joy cooed. "It is all right. It is all right."

The box also contained a single sheet of stationery, folded and pasted to the box's inside wall. Joy unfolded the note and, through her tears, read,

The Heart of Joy

Dearest Miss Joy,

I pray this little orphan finds a home in your heart. Her mother was crushed under a wagon's wheel, so she is alone in the world.

She is tiny but beautiful, is she not?

I am yours forever,

Edmund O'Dell

"Phone call for you, O'Dell," one of the agents called from the front of the Pinkerton office.

O'Dell sauntered to the phone mounted on the hallway wall and lifted the bell-like receiver. "O'Dell here."

Joy's voice stuttered and cracked over the wires. "G-good morning, Mr. O'Dell? Th-this is Joy Michaels calling. Could we, that is, would you care to c-call upon me this afternoon? And stay for dinner?"

Hope bloomed in O'Dell's chest, a flower unfurling to the light.

"Yes, I would. Very much so."

Joy answered the door herself, the diminutive scrap of a dog swaddled in flannel and tucked into the crook

The Heart of Joy

of her arm. The pup's eyes were creased in deep slumber.

"Good afternoon, Mr. O'Dell." Joy's greeting was timid, her smile tenuous.

He smiled back, drinking in her face, her hair, her eyes. Her sweet mouth.

Oh, thank you, Father! How I thank you!

What he answered Joy was, "Has she eaten for you?"

"I soaked the corner of a rag in sugar and milk, and she took right to it. She has eaten her fill three times today."

Joy led O'Dell into the parlor and closed the door behind them. Tea and cake were waiting on the little table between two chairs.

"I played hooky from work today to be with her." Joy gestured and O'Dell took a seat.

Joy took the chair opposite him. "Mr. O'Dell, I want to thank you for this precious gift. It made me think back and remember . . . that it was you who gave Blackie to me, more than five years ago . . . when we were living in Corinth."

The Heart of Joy

O'Dell nodded. "I am so sorry about Blackie, Miss Joy. I should have done more to save him."

Joy shook her head. "You did all anyone could have done, and more. You protected me, too. I-I apologize. It has been nearly two weeks and I never did thank you properly for putting yourself in harm's way for Blackie. For me. I-I must make amends."

She swallowed. "I thank you."

O'Dell's expression grew serious. "You must know, Miss Joy, that I would do anything—risk anything—to protect you."

Joy ducked her head. "Yes, I think I know that."

The conversation lapsed, and O'Dell shifted in his chair. "I see you have tea things laid out. I would volunteer to pour, but my left arm is still quite weak, and I might drop your cup. Would you like me to hold—have you given her a name?"

Joy chuckled. "Yes, but it is not terribly original. Her name is Blackie. Our—I mean *my*—third Blackie."

O'Dell laughed aloud, not intimidated by Joy's oblique and

unintentional reference to Grant. "Well, Blackie is easy to remember, is it not?"

He held out his good arm and Joy transferred the sleeping bundle to him.

"She feels nice," he remarked. "Warm and plump."

"Oh, but she is so tiny! That must be her greedy belly you feel. It is as tight as a drum." Joy poured tea for both of them, then took Blackie from O'Dell and resumed her seat.

She stirred cream into her cup and sighed. "I hardly know where to begin. Where do we go from here, Mr. O'Dell?"

He was silent for a moment. When he had sipped on his tea, he suggested, "Could you, that is, are you willing to express the objections you have toward me or concerning us, Miss Joy? I believe you have reservations and that they must weigh heavy upon your mind. I would like to hear you speak of them so that we can take them to the Lord. Together."

Joy sighed, now even more miserable.

The Heart of Joy

Take them to the Lord.

Together.

Why have I been unwilling to take my heart to you, Lord? I am so sorry.

Joy nodded and lifted sad eyes to him. "I suppose I should first apologize for writing that terrible note to you. It was neither mature nor kind of me. It had to have . . . wounded you, and I am sorry."

O'Dell nodded. "It did hurt, but if we are to be honest with each other, you and I are bound to injure each other's sensibilities from time to time, are we not?

I want to be a godly man, one who is quick to forgive, swift to cover offenses with Christ's love."

Joy blushed and looked down. "You are a younger Christian than I am, and yet your maturity shames me."

"Perhaps, but I care too deeply about you to allow unforgiveness to lodge in my heart. Ever."

Joy pondered what he said and was quiet for a while before she ventured, "You asked about my reservations."

The Heart of Joy

"Yes, and please do not hold back. I desire truthfulness between us."

"Thank you. I-I, well . . ." Joy cast about, looking for the right words, knowing that she had to speak her mind, as distasteful as the idea might be. If they were to have a future together, she had to be truthful.

"I-I suppose every woman hopes that the man she, um . . ."

"The man she marries?"

Joy sighed and nodded. "Yes, thank you. I suppose she hopes

that the gentleman can afford a wife and a . . . family."

O'Dell nodded. "Of course."

Joy twisted the napkin in her hand. "I-I have an income from my shop, of course, but should we, er, be blessed with ch—"

She could not say the word "children" and tried another tack. "I only bring this up because I accompanied Marshal Pounder to your rooms to retrieve your things when you were under our care."

That approach was no better, and Joy's mouth turned as dry as dirt. She stopped and sipped her

The Heart of Joy

tea, but it did not seem to help. She could not bring herself to voice her suspicion that O'Dell was in no position, financially, to marry.

O'Dell, for his part, was stumped. He fumbled in his mind to arrive at Joy's meaning.

I accompanied Marshal Pounder to your rooms.

A vivid picture of his bleak furnishings flashed before his eyes—and, in a rush, her concerns became clear. He could not help it; he started to chuckle.

And then laugh.

Joy blushed red to the roots of her wheat-blonde hair. "Really," she muttered. "I thought we had agreed to be frank. I did not comprehend that we would also be merry at each other's expense."

O'Dell ran the back of his hand across his eyes. It came away damp, and still he could not quite be sober.

"I do apologize, Joy." But he was grinning.

Joy. He called me Joy.

It had been years since O'Dell had called her by her first name. As a friend and while Grant was alive, he had done so; later he had reverted to 'Mrs. Michaels.'" As a suitor, he had been careful to address her as 'Miss Joy.'

The intimacy his change of address implied sent shivers through her. Then he reached across the little table. He took her hand in his. Joy shivered again.

"My rooms are less than, er, homey, do you not agree?" O'Dell's dark eyes danced. "When viewed from your perspective, my abode must have appeared well-nigh impoverished. So, may I share a little secret with you?"

Joy blinked and then nodded.

"I care not how I live as a bachelor, but I do care how I provide for a wife. For three years, I have lived in simple, straitened circumstances so that I might, out of my quite-adequate salary, salt away all I could afford. When I take a bride, I hope to bring her to a house I have already paid for, a house she will be proud to make our home."

"You-you have been saving for a house?"

O'Dell raised one brow. "Every spare nickel, dime, and dollar that has crossed my palm has gone into my savings account."

"Oh!" The news astounded Joy, and a warm, comfortable glow settled in the pit of her stomach.

And then his words echoed back to her. *For three years.*

He has been saving for three years? He has been saving to buy a house for us from the day Grant died?

The realization turned the warmth in her stomach sour.

O'Dell must have followed the direction of her thoughts as they flitted through her mind—and across her face. He flexed his jaw and, unwilling to let doubts and half-truths linger between them, chose to bring into the light the topic most painful to Joy.

"May we speak of Grant, Joy? May we speak of your late husband and my dearest friend?"

Joy looked away for a moment and then muttered, "I suppose. If we must."

O'Dell's words were rough. Blunt. "Grant knew."

Joy shook her head once and frowned. "He knew . . . he knew what?"

The Heart of Joy

"He knew how I felt about you. All along, he knew."

"How you felt?" Her frown deepened. "How can you—"

"Because he told me."

Joy ran her stiff, parched tongue over her lips. "I am not sure I comprehend."

"Then let me clarify so no doubt or uncertainty remains. Grant wrote to me and asked me to come to Denver for a visit. His request that I come was so insistent that I came at once. I had no knowledge of his illness until I arrived—the very morning your baby was born.

"That afternoon, after you had delivered your son, Grant asked to speak privately with me. I have kept his confidence for three years, but now you must know what he said."

In quiet words, O'Dell repeated the one-sided conversation. Echoing in his memories, he could hear Grant's voice—weak, yes, but strong in conviction.

Grant had leaned toward him. "*My friend, I don't have many months left to me. Will you help me?*"

The Heart of Joy

He had looked up, dreading what was coming. "Of course, Grant. Whatever it is."

And Grant had told him, ". . . because I am dying, Edmund O'Dell, my dearest friend, I must talk plainly: I know you once had feelings for Joy. Please do not protest. I knew this the first time I saw you look at her—while you still thought her a widow.

"I do not mention this in condemnation! Rather, I say this to one of the most honorable men I have had the privilege of knowing. I have never feared you, Mr. O'Dell,

because I know your worthy heart, just as I know that Joy's heart belongs to me. No, you did not dishonor me, and I say this to your credit, realizing the struggle you endured.

"Why did I write and ask you to come to Denver? Before it is too late, I wish you to make me a solemn promise, my friend. I wish you to promise me that when I am gone you will watch over Joy . . . In time, if it is God's will and when Joy's grief allows her to love again, I hope you will marry her . . ."

The Heart of Joy

O'Dell's black Irish eyes
moistened as he stared at Joy.
"I tell you these things only
because I desire you to be free,
Joy. Free from guilt, free from the
fear that you are betraying Grant.
Free to live again. To be happy."

A single tear hung upon Joy's
lashes and threatened to trickle
down her face, but she turned her
gaze upon O'Dell. "He-he said all
that? Truly?"

Something, partly sorrow,
partly release, flickered in her eyes.

"I affirm to you, most solemnly,
that he did."

Grant had said more, but O'Dell would share it with her at another juncture, in another place and time. This was not that place, and now was not that time.

"Edmund, I wish you to promise me that when I am gone you will watch over Joy and our son. In time, if it is God's will and when Joy's grief allows her to love again, I hope you will marry her . . . and raise my son—my son to whom I gave your name.

"I cannot think of any man I would wish to be a father to my son besides you! I say, 'if it is God's

will,' because the Lord will lead and guide you in this. I am content that, if you pray and follow his direction, all will be well.

"I am asking a difficult thing of you, my friend, I know—but it is so strong in my heart, and I sense death closing in on me. I cannot let what time I have left slip away without speaking to you and asking for your sincere word.

"Will you give me your word on this?"

Instead, O'Dell spoke to Joy from the depths of his soul. "Grant knew he was dying, Joy, and he knew you could not mourn him forever. He recognized that you had many years still to live after he passed, and he loved you too much to wish that you should spend them alone.

"And so, I have waited. I have waited and watched. As these three long, slow years have slipped by us, I believe—and you must tell me if I am correct in my assumptions— that you have come to think on me with some fondness? With affection? Have you, Joy?"

The Heart of Joy

Joy nodded, just a little, and that single, errant tear dripped from her chin.

O'Dell stood and maneuvered around the tea table to her side. He still held her hand in his.

"Then I must tell you, I must declare to you, that no man alive loves you as I do, Joy. And no other man alive knows and understands your love for Grant and your grief over losing him and Edmund. No man alive can honor them as I have—and as I will."

He slipped to one knee and clasped her hand to his chest. "I affirm my love for you. I wish to marry you and build a happy life with you. My darling, I wish to heal your grief-sick heart.

"Joy Thoresen Michaels, will you do me the great honor of becoming my wife?"

O'Dell froze—immobile—as he awaited her answer, but his heart thrummed in hopeful anticipation.

৵ ❈ ๙

Joy closed her eyes. The warmth and pressure of O'Dell's hand upon hers was bliss. Even with her emotions tossing and swirling her about, she clung to his hand and

The Heart of Joy

rehearsed the words O'Dell had spoken concerning Grant's wishes: "When Joy's grief allows her to love again, I hope you will marry her."

Oh, Grant! You foresaw this day? That I would need to love again? I always knew you were a great man, a godly man, but your love and care for me in your dying hours blesses me still.

And sets me free.

She opened her eyes. No more tears clouded her vision.

"Yes, Edmund O'Dell. I will be your wife."

"I love you, Joy Thoresen Michaels."

She smiled. "I receive your love and offer you mine."

The smile on O'Dell's face matched her own. He fumbled in the breast pocket of his suitcoat and drew out a circlet of gold sparkling with sapphires.

Joy inhaled. "Oh!"

"Joy, my beloved, will you accept this ring as the token of my intentions?"

"I—oh, yes!"

The Heart of Joy

He lifted her hand and slipped the ring on the third finger of her left hand.

Joy stared, not at the ring glinting on her hand, but at the man whose love shone brighter than any token.

"Oh, Edmund!"

"May I kiss you, Joy?"

Joy reddened and a slightly hysterical laugh burbled up in her chest. "Y-yes, but I-I have never . . . no one but Grant. Not ever."

"Then let us see how you like it, shall we?"

O'Dell took her face in his good hand and leaned toward her.

Joy closed her eyes and felt the warmth of his breath as his mouth neared hers.

His lips were firm, tender.

His kiss was *wonderful.* It—

Something fuzzy prickled her upper lip and her nose. She giggled.

O'Dell opened his eyes. Pulled back. Frowned.

"Was it that terrible?"

Joy grinned. "Not a bit! But your mustache—it tickles."

The Heart of Joy

"Ah! Then let us try again. See if you could grow to like it."

He leaned in and kissed her again, a little firmer, a little longer.

Joy sighed.

Oh, I like it, all right.

CHAPTER 7

Joy and O'Dell remained cloistered in the parlor for some time, talking and making plans. When they began to stir and think on the time, they were shocked to observe that the clock read 6:55. Dinner had commenced without them—and no one had knocked to call them to table.

No one had disturbed them.

"Do you think we should join them at this late juncture?" O'Dell asked. He had not released Joy's hand, where it curled comfortably in his. Where he wanted it always.

"I, well, I suppose we should . . ." Joy did not finish her thought.

"You supposed we should what, my dear?"

Joy liked how the 'my dear' O'Dell added to his question sounded. She liked it so much that she laughed a little.

And he knew.

He knew she liked it.

"You are 'my dear' now, you know." His dark eyes gleamed, and he leaned in to tease another kiss from her.

When—breathless—they drew apart, he asked again. "What should we do, my Joy?"

"Well, we should . . . we should tell them."

"I would be delighted to make the announcement, if you wish it. Do you wish it, Joy?"

She nodded. "Yes. Yes, please."

"Very well." O'Dell climbed to his feet and helped her to stand. He tucked her hand into the crook of his bandaged arm, and they made their way to the dining room.

The Heart of Joy

As Joy and O'Dell entered the dining room, the eyes of the diners turned toward them. No one spoke but hope and bright anticipation hung in the expressions of those seated.

O'Dell cleared his throat. "I should apologize to each of you for our tardiness to the dinner table. However, in lieu of an apology that, I confess, would be most insincere, I should prefer to make a happy announcement to all of you, our dearest friends and family.

"Just this evening, I have made Joy an offer of marriage," O'Dell turned his face toward Joy's and grinned, "and she . . . has accepted my proposal."

Happy pandemonium erupted in the dining room. No one cared about dinner any longer—with the exception of Will and Charley, who were awaiting dessert and could not be bothered with tedious "announcements"—not when chocolate cake was on the near horizon.

Rose hugged Joy first. "Oh, my darling daughter. I am so happy for you!"

The Heart of Joy

She then embraced O'Dell. "I shall be glad to call you my son," she whispered in his ear, "and I hope you will feel you can call me Mother."

O'Dell's eyes filled with moisture. He choked a little as he replied, "I had hoped to gain a wife. I had not dared to dream that I would gain a mother, too."

Rose placed a hand on his rough cheek. "From this day, you are my son."

O'Dell placed a kiss in her palm. "How I thank you, Miss Rose. *Mother.*"

O'Dell arrived at Palmer House after dinner the following evening. Joy, O'Dell, and Rose put their heads together to select a date and begin plans for the wedding.

"We were thinking of January," Joy said, "perhaps immediately following Christmas. A Sunday afternoon."

Rose retrieved a calendar from the wall by her desk. "Christmas is on a Friday this year and New Year's is the following Friday."

Joy's finger traced the dates and then she looked to O'Dell. "The first Sunday of the new year is January 3."

He nodded. "Since I cannot talk you into marrying me *this coming* Sunday, that date meets with my approval."

Joy and Rose laughed. Then Joy whispered, "January 3, then?"

O'Dell nodded. "Yes. In all practicality, I wish to have a home for us before we marry. A January date will give me just a bit more than six months to find, purchase, and furnish one. I will begin looking for a suitable house immediately.

Of course, I would like you to assist me in making the selection, Joy."

"Oh, yes! I should be delighted to." Joy turned to Rose in her excitement. "Just think, Mama, Edmund and I are to have our own home."

Rose nodded her approval, but her own thoughts had come to a crashing realization.

Oh, dear. I had not thought that Joy would be leaving Palmer House. She and Grant had lived here . . . but, of course, a similar arrangement will not suit. Joy and her new

The Heart of Joy

husband cannot live in the same cottage she and Grant lived in.

Joy noticed Rose's frozen smile. "Mama? Is something wrong?"

"No. No, dear, only that I just realized . . . you will be leaving us. And, of course, that is as it should be."

O'Dell glanced from mother to daughter but kept his silence.

Joy murmured, "We will be close, Mama. Still here in Denver."

"Oh, yes. Certainly. Please do not be concerned. I will adjust, and the Lord will raise up another helper for me."

Rose, not wishing to dampen Joy and O'Dell's happiness, was quick to change the subject. She turned to O'Dell. "Edmund, Tabitha is graduating from nursing school next week. Breona, Joy, and I had planned to attend. Would you care to accompany us to Boulder to celebrate her commencement and fetch her home?"

"I would be most happy to. Consider my automobile at your disposal."

"That would be wonderful. We shall make our arrangements accordingly."

The Heart of Joy

Rose turned to Joy. "Now, back to planning your wedding. Where would you like it to be held?"

Joy glanced at O'Dell before answering. "Here, we think. Our church is lovely, but an old warehouse is not exactly the ideal venue for a wedding nor is it the intimate setting we would prefer. We desire only a simple, sacred ceremony, officiated by Pastor Carmichael and surrounded by our friends and family, right here in the great room of Palmer House."

Rose smiled and nodded. "What a lovely idea! I quite agree, and I know all your friends here will decorate the house for you."

The next weeks and months sped by. Palmer House's beloved Tabitha graduated nursing school with the pomp and celebration she deserved. She returned home to Denver and to Palmer House and, mid-summer, took up a position at the Denver hospital.

Life at Palmer House was again as it should be.

Over the summer, O'Dell and Joy Rose viewed several houses on the Denver market, but they did

not immediately find one that met
with their satisfaction.

"We have time," O'Dell assured
Joy. "We have several months yet."

"Yes; I am certain the Lord will
lead us to the right one," Joy
replied.

In the meantime, her shop
downtown and his responsibilities
with the Pinkertons kept them both
busy. The evenings when they could
meet grew sweeter as they relaxed
into their affianced status and looked
forward to their wedding and the
start of their married state.

Vikki Kestell

On the second Saturday in October, after weeks of searching and viewing many houses, O'Dell and Joy found their dream home—a medium-sized, two-story dwelling, sound in structure but in need of repairs. Joy thought the house full of charm and possibility. As an added bonus, the house was located only a half mile from Palmer House.

"With a little work, it will be perfect, Edmund," Joy assured him.

"I agree! And the price is just right. In fact, we shall have a little

236

left over with which to begin the most necessary repairs."

They smiled at each other, happy in their prospects, growing in their love for each other.

"Will you make an offer on it, then?"

"On Monday. I should like to pray over it first."

"I will pray with you, Edmund. It is a big step."

O'Dell called for Joy the following morning to drive her to church. He extended an invitation to Rose, too, but she declined.

"The walk to church with the others each week does me a world of good," she said, laughing. "And someone must go along with the Palmer House contingency to keep our little ducks in a row, no?"

She did not mention the times in past years when the girls of Palmer House feared being snatched from their two-by-two ranks by the men from whom they had escaped. Billy was their greatest defense against such threats, but Rose was their fearless captain.

The Heart of Joy

Eventually all the residents of Palmer House arrived that morning at the old brick warehouse where Calvary Temple met for services. The Palmer House group filled four rows of six seats in the center section of the congregation, and O'Dell was proud to take his place next to Joy, proud to sit beside her, announcing to the world that they were an engaged couple.

That morning, after thirty minutes of uplifting songs of worship, Pastor Carmichael introduced the head of a Denver orphanage. The man stepped from the congregation where a raft of children of all ages occupied an entire section of old benches, odd chairs, and any seating the church could employ.

The orphanage's director, a Mr. Stephens, spoke with eloquence on the ministry—and needs—of the orphanage.

"At present, we are housing and educating seventy-two children," Mr. Stephens told the congregation. "Thanks to God's grace and your generous donations, we are making the lives of these children bearable and are showing them how much

The Heart of Joy

Jesus loves them. God willing, many of our children will find loving, adoptive parents; if they do not, they will grow to adulthood with good educations, prepared to make their own way in the world."

Mr. Stephens looked with fondness over the people of Calvary Temple. "We only need a little more help with food, my dear friends. Growing children need good food. If you are able to aid us, I promise that we will put your funds to good use."

Joy and O'Dell looked at each other. O'Dell opened his wallet and

Joy her purse. They gave what they had with gladness.

Monday morning, the bell over the door of *Michaels' Fine Furnishings* jingled, and Joy glanced up to greet a customer. Instead, she saw Edmund O'Dell.

"Good morning, my darling! I had not expected to see you this morning. Are you on your way to make the offer on our house?"

In place of a joyous greeting, O'Dell's brow creased. "Could you spare a minute to talk, Joy? In private?"

The Heart of Joy

Concerned, Joy nodded. "Of course. Let us go to my office."

With the door closed for privacy, O'Dell took Joy's hands in his. "I must tell you something, Joy, something that may hurt you a bit."

Joy blinked in surprise. "What is it, Edmund?"

"Well, I . . . I felt that the Lord spoke something to my heart, a thing I was to do."

"Then, of course, you must do it."

"Yes, but it will mean a significant change in our circumstances, Darling."

"Oh." Joy's heart thumped a little harder. "But, still, if it is what the Holy Spirit is directing you to do . . . Can you not tell me what it is?"

"Certainly. I will never keep anything from you." He gathered himself. "You know the orphan children who attend Calvary Temple with us?"

"Yes." Joy wondered where O'Dell was going.

Is he thinking for us to adopt? Is adoption what my father's blessing portended?

The Heart of Joy

She was distracted by her thoughts and unprepared for what he said next.

O'Dell sighed. "Last night, the orphanage's main dormitory burned to the ground."

"No! We had not heard. Oh, dear! What happened? Were any of the children harmed?"

O'Dell, because of his close connections to Denver law enforcement, often received news before the papers reported it. "I heard from Chief Groves that the furnace malfunctioned. It overheated and caught a joist afire.

The workers at the orphanage managed to remove all the children in time, but the fire took the entire dormitory."

"I do thank the Lord that there were no injuries—but what will they do?" Joy asked. "We already know how hard-pressed they are to keep the children in food and clothing."

O'Dell sighed again. "Yes, well, that is it . . ."

Joy saw "it" in a flash. *When I take a bride, I hope to bring her to a house I have already paid for, a house she will be proud to make our home . . . Every spare nickel,*

dime, and dollar that has crossed
my palm has gone into my savings
account.

"The money you have saved for
our house?"

He nodded. "I was on my way
to make the offer. My thoughts
were preoccupied with one thing:
how glad and proud I would be to
bring you to our own home when
we marry—how happy this house
would make us."

"And then?"

"And then while I walked along,
it was as though everything about
me grew hushed and quiet, as if

preparing for a great and
momentous announcement. I
actually stopped on the sidewalk
and stood still.

"*What, Lord*? I asked."

He took another deep breath.
"At once, a Scripture came to mind.
I have been studying God's word on
marriage, you see, and had
recently read Chapter 10 in the
Gospel of Mark. The chapter also
contained these verses:

"*And Jesus answered and said,*
Verily I say unto you,
There is no man that hath left
house, or brethren, or sisters,

The Heart of Joy

or father, or mother,

or wife, or children, or lands,

for my sake, and the gospel's,

But he shall receive an hundredfold

now in this time, houses, and

brethren, and sisters, and mothers,

and children, and lands,

with persecutions;

and in the world to come

eternal life.

"I felt the Lord ask in my spirit,
Are you willing to leave your house
for me? For my sake and the sake
of my gospel? I knew then that he
was asking me to give our house
money to rebuild the dormitory."

Her voice a little tremulous, Joy asked, "And what did you answer?"

O'Dell looked her full in the face. "I told the Lord that I would do as he asked."

Joy said nothing for a long moment. Then she squeezed his hand. "Edmund, we have committed ourselves and our marriage to God. If you had answered the Lord's request any differently, how could I continue to respect you as the godly man I have come to know? My papa—the man whose walk with the Lord I have admired the most—taught me that when our great God speaks, we must obey."

His grip on her hands tightened. "Thank you, Joy, for being the godly woman I fell in love with."

After a long moment of reflection, Joy asked, "Where, then, shall we live when we marry?"

O'Dell took a deep breath. "We shall pray for the Lord to show us a good house to rent. However, we will not always need to rent a house, Joy; there is nothing wrong with owning our own home. This sacrifice will only delay it for a few years."

"Yes, Edmund. Wherever we are together will be home to me."

They embraced, and Joy was not ashamed of the few tears she shed as she released to the God of Grace the perfect house that was to have been their home.

I give you everything, Lord, she prayed against O'Dell's shoulder. *All over again, I give you everything—everything! And how I thank you for this man I can trust to faithfully follow you.*

The Heart of Joy

"Where would you like these boxes, Miss Joy?" Billy asked. His arms held three crates—balanced precariously atop each other.

Joy came back to the present with a start. Inhaling the scent of spruce once more, she smiled and studied the boxes Billy carried. Joy knew what the boxes contained— shiny, glimmering ornaments, tree trimmings, and the wonderful and novel electric lights Martha Palmer had gifted to Palmer House a few Christmases ago.

Mr. Wheatley appeared behind Billy with two smaller boxes. One of the two boxes contained the manger scene so precious to them all.

As Joy's grin widened, Billy grinned back.

"It is good to see you happy again, Miss Joy."

"Thank you. It *is* good to feel alive . . . after so long."

"Our boys are nearly beside themselves in anticipation of Christmas morning," he told her.

"I quite understand. Will you place the boxes on the floor under the windows?"

Billy and Mr. Wheatley stacked their burdens along the wall as Joy had directed and left to bring down another load.

Joy perused the crates, looking for the one that held the crèche. She saw it, shifted one carton aside, took her prize to the sofa, and placed it on the low table before her.

Billy and Mr. Wheatley eventually returned with the remaining decorations. Billy picked up a small claw hammer.

"Would you like me to open them for you?"

"Yes, please. Could you start with this one?"

Vikki Kestell

Billy slid the hammer's claw under one end of the lid and pried it open. Seconds later, he removed the tacked-on lid.

Joy spied the manger scene within the straw padding inside the box. With care, she lifted the many swaddled pieces out one by one, unwrapped them, and set them on the table. Last of all came the manger itself.

Joy picked up the tiny infant Jesus and held it. *This will be my last Christmas at Palmer House. Next year Edmund and I will be decorating our own home for*

The Heart of Joy

Christmas . . . and perhaps we will be expecting a little one ourselves?

She sighed and squeezed her eyes closed. *O Lord! I thank you for bringing me out of the darkness of grief and into the light of a new love and hope. Truly, there is a time and a season for everything.*

CHAPTER 8

Christmas—with all its delight and celebration—was over. Joy and O'Dell's wedding was mere days away. They were to be married the Sunday afternoon following New Year's Day after church services.

Early Saturday, the girls of Palmer House, led by Breona and aided by Billy and Mr. Wheatley, cleared away the Christmas greenery and threw themselves into a scrupulous cleaning of the first floor. The busy workgroup removed

The Heart of Joy

drapes, trudged through the
January snow, shook the drapes,
and hung them on the frigid
clotheslines to air. They dusted
walls and ceilings and scrubbed
mantels and hearths.

Billy and Mr. Wheatley rolled
and removed carpets, taking them
out-of-doors for a thorough
beating. Once the carpets were out
of the way, the women swept and
cleaned the floors, waxing the
hardwood planks and rubbing them
until their arms ached and the
wood glowed.

They cleaned the gaslight fixtures and wiped their globes; they washed every window until the glass gleamed and met with Breona's approval. They polished furniture and rehung the drapes. Finally, they festooned the windows, walls, and doorways with the costly greens and hothouse flowers Martha Palmer had insisted upon ordering and sending to them.

The girls stood back, admiring their combined efforts and breathing in the lily-perfumed air.

"It will be so beautiful for them," Sarah smiled.

The Heart of Joy

"Aye. That it will." It was all Breona could muster. With the corner of her apron, she dabbed at her eyes.

❧ ✻ ☙

Later the same day, under a bright winter sun, Joy and O'Dell drove to Riverside Cemetery. Their closest friends met them there.

Together, Joy and O'Dell placed a garland of flowers upon the simple grave of Grant Michaels. Joy wept unabashedly—tears of sorrow but tears of healing, too.

When she placed her hand upon Grant's headstone, O'Dell, with his hand covering Joy's, whispered, "Grant, my dearest friend, you already know that I am doing my best to fulfill my promises to you. Joy and I will stand before God tomorrow and make our solemn vows of marriage, but we do not forget you . . . and we do not forget Edmund. When we find your sweet boy, I will fulfill my pledge to you to raise him as my own."

❦❀❧

On the drive back to Palmer House, O'Dell squeezed Joy's hand.

"Tomorrow you shall be my wife—Joy

The Heart of Joy

Thoresen O'Dell. I am beyond happy, my love."

"As am I, Edmund."

"And you are satisfied with the little cottage I have rented to begin our married life?"

Joy smiled. "I am satisfied that, wherever I lay my head, yours will be on the pillow next to mine."

"You are perfect, Joy."

"No, Edmund, only our great God is perfect. I am content to live within his perfect love and care."

O'Dell's grin grew larger. "Like I said. You are perfect."

Vikki Kestell

Sunday afternoon, January 3, 1915, Joy and Edmund O'Dell came together in the great room of Palmer House and joined right hands. Rose stood with her daughter, and Mr. Wheatley stood with O'Dell. The room overflowed with their family and friends.

Into the holy hush, Isaac Carmichael placed one hand upon their joined hands and blessed them. "Edmund and Joy, I now pronounce you husband and wife. Therefore, what God has joined together, let no man put asunder."

POSTSCRIPT

CHRISTMAS 1917

Rose slipped from O'Dell and Joy's bedroom into the hall and walked the short distance to the little living room of their rented house. She found her son-in-law sitting on the sofa, his arms propped upon his legs, his face on his hands.

Where he had been for eight hours.

"Edmund."

O'Dell's chin snapped up.

"Edmund, you may come in, now," Rose beckoned O'Dell toward the bedroom.

O'Dell stood and was surprised at how shaky his legs were. *I have faced off with the worst kinds of criminals, confronted death a number of times, yet I am undone by this common event?*

But there was nothing common about the life and wellbeing of his precious wife.

"Is Joy all right? Is the baby here at last?"

"Come see for yourself."

The Heart of Joy

O'Dell stumbled after Rose and followed her into the bedroom. Dr. Murphy, standing at the bedside, beamed at him, but said nothing. He and Rose tiptoed from the room, leaving O'Dell alone with Joy.

"Joy? Are you all right?"

The smile overspreading her face should have told him everything, but he wanted—*he needed*—to hear her say it.

"Yes, my love. I am well— thanks be to God."

O'Dell came closer. A tiny bundle lay in the crook of Joy's arm.

"Our baby?"

"We have a son, Edmund."

O'Dell reeled at the news. He plunked into a nearby chair. "We have a son!"

Joy laughed. Her laughter was full and free, filled with promise and with hope. With love.

"Come and see your son, Papa."

O'Dell scooted the chair as close to the bed as he could, and Joy turned back the corner of the blanket. Within its folds lay a red, wrinkled little man, whose black eyes were wide—looking but not yet seeing, searching but not yet finding. The babe's mouth opened a

The Heart of Joy

little, and he emitted a single
squawk.

"What!" O'Dell was entranced.
He stared at the tiny face with a
hunger he'd never known.

"May I . . . May I hold him?"

"Of course." Joy pushed herself
up in the bed and lifted the baby
with practiced ease. "Put out your
arms, Papa Edmund. No, together.
Like this."

O'Dell received the blanketed
bundle and was amazed at how
light it was as it rested in his
arms—and yet how shaky his arms
were under its negligible weight.

He leaned toward the child and studied him as he had never studied any human creature. "He is so . . ."

O'Dell could not find the right word. Sporting a flattened nose and a smattering of black hair on the top of his head, the infant was neither comely nor beautiful—not that O'Dell could boast of previous encounters with newborns. No, he had nary a single experience with which he might compare this one. And yet . . .

"Yes? He is so?"

"He is so . . ."

The Heart of Joy

Again O'Dell struggled to put into words how the ruddy, crinkled face and wizened dark eyes affected him.

O'Dell looked up and into Joy's face. "He is a miracle."

There. He had found the right word. And it *was* the best, the most apt descriptor, for O'Dell was in awe.

Joy smiled her approval and caressed the dark hair that crowned the baby's head. "What is our son's name, Edmund? Oh, and Merry Christmas, my darling."

O'Dell shook his head. "I beg your pardon?"

"It is Christmas morning, dearest. Our son is born on Christmas Day."

"Christmas! I-I suppose I have been preoccupied."

Joy's laughter rang in the room and in his heart. "*You* have been preoccupied? That is rich."

He grinned. "I take your point. So, Christmas? His birthday will be Christmas?"

"Yes, Edmund. From here forward."

The Heart of Joy

"And our little miracle will require a name?"

"Um, yes. I believe it is customary to name one's children."

They laughed, and O'Dell knew his heart had never been so full, so enriched and content. "My father's name was Matthew. I did not know him well; he died when I was still a young lad. However, he was a good man—a good husband and father."

"Ah! Matthew is a Biblical name meaning *Gift of God*. So, Matthew O'Dell?"

He tried it, too. "Matthew O'Dell. I like it. He is certainly our gift from God. What about a middle name?"

"I leave it to you, Edmund."

O'Dell studied the babe in his arms. The child's eyes had drifted closed, but in sleep, the babe's little lips remained parted. His tiny chest rose and fell in a soft, regular rhythm.

Matthew. My son! Matthew O'Dell, I could watch you forever, O'Dell found to his surprise.

Ah, Lord! How I thank you for this great gift, this son.

O'Dell looked up at Joy.

The Heart of Joy

"Perhaps something from your side of the family?"

She nodded.

O'Dell looked at their son and then back at Joy. "What do you think of Matthew Thoresen O'Dell?"

Still smiling, Joy closed her eyes against the sting of sudden tears. She blinked away the moisture. "Thank you, Edmund."

Her husband's dark eyes studied Joy with an intensity that warmed her. He took her hand. "No, thank *you*, my darling Joy, for the most precious Christmas gift I have ever received."

Vikki Kestell

He placed their joined hands on the sleeping infant.

"My son, you are Matthew Thoresen O'Dell—a gift to us from God, our Father. We commit to raise you well, nurturing you in the love and admonition of our Lord. May you know and serve the Savior all the days of your life. Amen."

Joy responded, "Oh, amen! May it ever be so, Lord."

ABOUT
THE AUTHOR

Vikki Kestell's passion for people and their stories is evident in her readers' affection for her characters and unusual plotlines. Two often-repeated sentiments are, "I feel like I know these people," and "I am right there, in the book, experiencing what her characters experience."

Vikki holds a PhD in organizational learning and instructional technologies. She left a career of twenty-plus years in government, academia, and corporate life to pursue writing full time. "Writing is the best job ever," she admits, "and the most demanding."

Vikki and her husband, Conrad Smith, make their home in Albuquerque, New Mexico.

Want to receive new book release notifications? Sign up for Vikki's newsletter on her website, **http://www.vikkikestell.com**, or follow her on Facebook, BookBub, and Goodreads.

BOOKS BY VIKKI KESTELL

A PRAIRIE HERITAGE

Book 1: *A Rose Blooms Twice*
Book 2: *Wild Heart on the Prairie*
Book 3: *Joy on This Mountain*
Book 4: *The Captive Within*
Book 5: *Stolen*
Book 6: *Lost Are Found*
Book 7: *All God's Promises*
Book 8: *The Heart of Joy* (A Short Story)
Book 9: *Rose of RiverBend*

GIRLS FROM THE MOUNTAIN

Book 1: *Tabitha* (also in audio)
Book 2: *Tory*
Book 3: *Sarah Redeemed*

LAYNIE PORTLAND

Book 1: *Laynie Portland, Spy Rising*
Book 2: *Laynie Portland, Retired Spy*
Book 3: *Laynie Portland, Renegade Spy*
Book 4: *Laynie Portland, Spy Resurrected*

NANOSTEALTH (ALSO IN AUDIO)

Book 1: *Stealthy Steps*
Book 2: *Stealth Power*
Book 3: *Stealth Retribution*
Book 4: *Deep State Stealth*

Made in the USA
Coppell, TX
14 January 2021

48157781R00157